THE HEIR'S FORTUNE

RECKLESS ROGUES
BOOK FIVE

ELLIE ST. CLAIR

♥ **Copyright 2024 Ellie St Clair**

All rights reserved.

This book or parts thereof may not be reproduced in any form, stored in any retrieval system, or transmitted in any form by any means—electronic, mechanical, photocopy, recording, or otherwise—without prior written permission of the publisher.

Facebook: Ellie St. Clair

Cover by AJF Designs

Do you love historical romance? Receive access to a free ebook, as well as exclusive content such as giveaways, contests, freebies and advance notice of pre-orders through my mailing list!

Sign up here!

Reckless Rogues
The Earls's Secret
The Viscount's Code
The Scholar's Key
The Lord's Compass
The Heir's Fortune

For a full list of all of Ellie's books, please see
www.elliestclair.com/books.

INTRODUCTION

Dear reader,

Before you embark on the fifth and final story of the Reckless Rogues, I would like to take a quick moment to reacquaint you with our characters.

While The Heir's Fortune can be read as a standalone, I highly recommend that you read the books in this series in order, for there is an overarching plot that will be much more enjoyable that way.

The characters from the previous books all make an appearance in this one.

You can find them featured in each book, as follows:

1. The Earls's Secret
    Lady Cassandra Sutcliffe
    Devon Addison, Lord Covington

2. The Viscount's Code
    Lady Hope Newfield
    Anthony Davonport, Viscount Whitehall

INTRODUCTION

3. The Scholar's Key
    Lady Persephone (Percy) Holloway
    Mr. Noah Rowley

4. The Lord's Compass
    Lady Faith Newfield
    Eric Rowley, Lord Ferrington

5. The Heir's Fortune
    Lady Madeline Bainbridge
    Gideon Sutcliffe, Lord Ashford

Enjoy.

Ellie

CHAPTER 1

"Come on out, now, no need to be shy."
Gideon stretched his hand as far as he could while using the other to try to inch himself forward, but it was no use – he wasn't going to fit in the hollowed-out tree trunk that lay across the path of the ruins before him.

The dog at the other end whimpered and shrunk away from him, still shivering. Gideon sighed as he let his arm go limp, wishing he had an enticing piece of food on him to draw the dog out, for alas, the dog found him as unremarkable as everyone else did.

"I promise if you come with me, I will take you to the kitchen, and the Cook will give you all of the scrap meat you'd like. I cannot say it will be particularly well-prepared, but you do not have high standards, do you now?"

The dog — either a pup or a small breed — Gideon couldn't tell from where he was, tilted its head to the side, one ear flopping over as though he was listening to him and considering his words.

"I cannot leave you out here but I am becoming rather chilled," Gideon said, holding his hand out again, palm up, and the dog leaned its head forward, sniffing. "There we go—"

"What are you doing?"

Gideon jumped, the voice startling him, causing him to hit his head on the top of the log.

"Damn it," he said, lifting a hand to the sore spot as the dog whimpered and drew away from him once more.

Gideon shuffled backward, squinting up to see the figure towering over him in front of the now-setting sun, arms crossed over her chest as her cloak billowed in the cold wind behind her.

He knew that shape. It was one of his sister's friends — her closest friend, if he was correct, and the one he tried the hardest to avoid.

"Lady Madeline?" he said, trying to contain his groan as he rubbed his head. "You startled me."

"Clearly," she said, looking around. "I almost passed by you, but I must admit that my curiosity as to why a future duke was on his belly, his bottom in the air as he crawled into a log in the middle of the forest was just too overwhelming to continue on without learning more. Please, you must explain."

"So that you can tell this story to our friends for your amusement?" he snorted. "I think not."

"I shall be telling it one way or another, so you might as well provide me with your side of things."

"Fine," he said, opening his mouth to explain his dilemma, but just as he did, a whine resounded.

"What was that?" Lady Madeline asked, looking from one side to the other, her silky dark hair that had fallen out of most of its pins floating around her face.

"That," Gideon said with exasperation, "is what I am trying to save."

She arched an eyebrow but instead of demanding more

information or retreating at the idea of a wild animal as most women would, she rounded the other side of the log, crouching down without care that her knee was resting on the damp ground before standing with the puppy in her arms, its dirty and matted fur spoiling her cloak and gown underneath.

"Is this who you were trying so hard to catch?" she asked as she nuzzled her face against the dog's fur.

"Yes," Gideon said, unable to mask his annoyance as he stood, brushing dirt and dried leaves off his breeches. "Two people being here clearly made it much easier to convince the pup to come out."

"Or maybe he just likes me better," Madeline said with a grin before lifting the puppy in front of her to inspect him. "Who is he?"

"I am not sure," Gideon said, lifting his hands to the side. "I was walking around the ruins and heard a noise so I came to investigate. That's when I found him."

"Poor thing," she said. "My best guess is that he is a couple of months old, which means he is old enough to have left his mama but I wouldn't say he could survive long on his own."

"I doubt it," Gideon agreed, stepping toward Lady Madeline and the dog. She was his sister's closest friend and had spent a great deal of time at Castleton, and yet, he didn't know her very well. She was so forward and apt to say the most unlikely comments that he always avoided her if he could, for she put him on edge.

He reached out a hand and hesitantly ran it down the dog's back, surprised when the puppy leaned into his touch with a whimper.

Lady Madeline looked up at him in surprise, and a tremble ran down Gideon's spine at her proximity. A tremble from… uneasiness? He never knew what to expect from this woman – and he did not like surprises.

"Maybe he doesn't mind you so much after all," she said with a laugh as the puppy licked his hand. "What were you doing out here, anyway?"

"Seeing to my lands," he said guardedly, uncertain why he needed to have an excuse to wander his own property.

"You weren't searching for treasure?" she asked with a sly smile over the dog's head.

"Would it matter if I was?" he asked defensively. "I have every right to do so."

"Steady there, I was just asking," she said with what seemed to be a roll of her eyes. "Do you take everything so seriously?"

"Everything that matters," he said, watching her black cloak swirl in the wind. "We should be getting back. The sun is lowering."

"What about the dog?" she asked, lifting the bundle in her arms, and he crooked his fingers toward her.

"I'll take him."

She stepped backward so that they were both out of reach, fixing him with a hard stare. "Where are you going to take him?"

"To the stables," he said, becoming annoyed now. "Where would you think I would take him?"

She bit her lip, her normally stoic façade loosening its grip, allowing him to see a different side of her.

"He's so small and has been out here all alone," she said. "Do you not think he should come to the house?"

Gideon took a breath, lifting a hand in the air. "He chose to come to you, so I suppose you can do with him what you'd like."

She was already shaking her head. "I cannot have a dog."

"Why not?"

She shrugged her shoulders. "I am not one to make much

commitment to anything. I cannot keep a dog when I do not know where I might be living in a short time."

Gideon cocked his head to the side as he stared at the two of them. "He doesn't seem to understand that."

Nor did Gideon, but he wasn't about to ask questions. Madeline looked down at the dog, a moment of vulnerability crossing over her face before she shoved the dog toward him. "Here," she said. "Take him. He's yours."

Gideon softened, seeing how much this had affected her.

"I'll take him to the stables, but only to be cleaned up, and then he can come inside," he said. "We shall see what my mother thinks of him."

"Of course," Lady Madeline said, giving a curt nod. "I should be going."

"I will walk you back," he said. "You shouldn't be out here alone."

"I shouldn't," she said. "But I am anyway."

And with that, she strode off, fast enough to make him aware that she would prefer he did not follow.

She was a mystery that one. But one mystery that wasn't up to him to solve.

Try as he might to concentrate on anything other than Lady Madeline, she was still on Gideon's mind when Cassandra found him in his study a few hours later, the dog at his feet, curled up on a pillow that had previously been perched upon one of the parlor sofas. He hoped his mother wouldn't note its absence, or, if she did, she would forgive him. She was currently upstairs visiting with his father and had yet to notice the dog.

"Oh, there he is!"

Gideon looked up at his sister's voice, surprised that she

was so excited to see him, but when she ran in to crouch beside the dog, he realized that she wasn't talking to him at all. She reached down to let the puppy lick her face.

"Where is your baby?" Gideon asked, more curious than perturbed. Since the young lad had been born, Cassandra had spent far more time with her son than most other women of her station would with their offspring. Gideon actually admired her for it.

"He's with Madeline," she said, and Gideon found himself rather piqued at her friend's name, but before he could ask any more, Devon – Lord Covington, Cassandra's husband, and Gideon's closest friend – followed his wife in the door.

"I heard there was a pup in here," he said, looking around the room. "Has he made a mess all over the floor yet?"

"Not yet," Gideon said. "A footman has seen to his requirements."

"Good to hear it," Devon said with a grin. "Perhaps you will make a proud papa after all."

Gideon snorted, bending his head so that Devon and Cassandra wouldn't see his face. Despite being closer to him than any other two people in the world, he didn't want them to see how much the words affected him.

For it was true – he *would* like to be a father. He just wasn't sure when — or if — that day would ever come.

"It is unfortunate that Hope, Faith, Percy, and their husbands have left," Cassandra said as she stroked the dog, whose fur was rather soft now that it had been properly washed. "They would have loved him."

"I'd like to see Whitehall with a dog," Devon said with a laugh, referencing the rather ill-natured Lord Whitehall, who had married Lady Hope.

The five men who had been part of their group that undertook daring adventures had joined Gideon on a quest when he had found a riddle that he assumed would lead to a treasure. His sister had found another copy of the same riddle, leading her and her four closest friends to start their own hunt. Eventually, they merged their efforts after Cassandra and Devon fell in love while solving the first riddle, which had only led to another clue instead of the treasure Gideon had been hoping for.

"Whitehall might be a genius codebreaker, which helped us a great deal when it came to solving the second clue, but an animal man, I cannot see," Gideon said, leaning back, no longer attempting the pretense of continuing his work.

The code Whitehall had solved with the help of Lady Hope had led to a third clue, one which required retrieving a necklace from Gideon and Cassandra's aunt in Bath. As Lady Percy was there at the same time as Noah Rowley, they had undertaken the search together, which ended in finding a clue within the necklace – and marriage to one another.

Rowley's brother, Lord Ferrington, had then traveled to Spain along with a stowaway, Lady Faith, and they had returned with a map as well as a marriage due to their compromising situation. Fortunately, it had led to love in the end.

As for the map? Gideon now had it in his possession and was doing his damnedest to determine where it led.

"What were you doing in the ruins, anyway?" Cassandra asked. "The last time we were there, Devon knocked over a wall and we were both nearly injured."

"But aren't you glad we were?" Devon asked, grinning suggestively at his wife, which had Gideon leaning back in his chair and shaking his head.

"I was getting impatient," he said. "I know we need to take a better look at the map together and solve the path it will be leading us down, but I couldn't help the urge to begin searching myself."

"That's how you will get in trouble, Gideon," Cassandra

said, straightening. "All of us who have gone after a clue have found ourselves in danger at one time or another."

"Is that why you are still here?" Gideon asked with sinking dread in his stomach. "I wondered why you hadn't left yet. I had assumed that you wanted to stay to see this through, but is it because you do not think I am capable of accomplishing this alone?"

"Of course you are more than capable," Cassandra said, rising from the floor where the dog had returned to his slumber and taking a chair in front of Gideon's desk, crossing her arms over her chest. "We are still here for a few reasons. One being that I wanted Mother to be able to spend time with the baby."

"And we do want to see this thing through, that part is true. We started this and we would like to see it to the finish," Devon added, exchanging a meaningful look with his wife.

"And also…" Cassandra said, slightly wincing as she did so, "We hate to see you all alone."

"Mother and Father are both here, and I have been alone for years," Gideon said, his spine straightening. "I am more than capable of looking after myself."

"You can look after yourself, but do you want to?" Cassandra asked imploringly. "No one *wants* to be alone."

"Some of us have to be happy doing so," he said uncomfortably, for his statement was not entirely true.

"Will you not seek out a wife?" she asked, shifting forward in her seat, her blue eyes boring into him.

"In due time," Gideon said, exasperated with this conversation, but he did feel that he owed an explanation to the two of them. "I cannot offer a woman marriage when we live in such ruins."

"Castleton is hardly a ruin," Devon said, leaning back against the doorframe as he studied him. Devon had helped Gideon through some difficult times in his life, and likely knew what he was thinking better than anyone. "Yes, it could use some improvements, but when I tell you that it is comfortable and I enjoy my time here, I mean it."

"We need servants, we need improvements, we need furniture that wasn't built for my great-grandfather!" Gideon said, throwing his hands into the air. "I'd like to offer a woman more than this. I have rested my hopes on this treasure for over a year now. However... if this treasure comes to nothing – and I am beginning to think that might be the case – then I might have less choice as to who I marry."

"What is that supposed to mean?" Cassandra asked, her head snapping up, and she had to push back a piece of hair, the same auburn color as his own, away from her face.

"It means," he said carefully, "that if there is no other option, I will have to marry a woman with a significant dowry."

Cassandra bit her lip. "Gideon, that is so sad."

He shrugged. "It's practical."

"Yes, but—"

"It is what it is, Cassandra," he said, not wanting to speak on it any longer.

"You know, I had always wondered if maybe Madeline—"

"No," he said swiftly, holding up a hand.

"Why would you not even entertain the idea?" she asked defensively, which made sense, for Cassandra was as loyal of a friend as there ever was.

"Madeline's family would want nothing to do with the scandals that come with ours."

"How can you say that?" Cassandra said indignantly. "For one, her family is not exactly conventional nor concerned about scandal. Her father has provided her more freedom than any father should, and he would be thrilled to have her married off to any eligible young man. Secondly, you just finished saying that you will marry for a fortune if you have to."

"Of which, if I am not mistaken, Madeline has none."

"That is true. But if we find the treasure, that doesn't matter. Why would you be willing to saddle another unsuspecting young woman with our family scandal and not Madeline?"

Gideon knew that his words were not going to be accepted by Cassandra, but he owed her the truth.

"Madeline is not the type of woman to sit back and allow scandal to ebb away."

"What does that mean?"

"It means... that she has a propensity to say what she thinks without worrying about the consequences. I would like to lead our family back to respectability."

"That is a most terrible thing to say," Cassandra said, standing abruptly. "But perhaps I forgot the lengths you are willing to go to in order to make things so respectable."

"Cassandra..."

Cassandra just glared at him, and Gideon was reminded of how angry she had been with him for so many years. He had made mistakes in his past — mistakes that had led to her being ostracized for sins that she didn't even commit — and he thought they had moved past them.

But perhaps she had only forgiven him and not forgotten.

"Well," Cassandra said, stepping backward toward Devon, who appeared rather ill-at-ease, caught between his wife and his closest friend, "whatever you do, do not let Mother or Father know of your plan. They would be devastated."

"Why?" Gideon said, raking a hand through his hair. "It is their fault we are in this mess."

"Gideon!"

He sighed, lowering his head. "I know. That was a beastly thing to say. It was not the fault of either of them."

"No, it certainly was not," Cassandra said.

"It was my fault," Gideon muttered in a low voice, admitting out loud for the first time the thought that had haunted him for years now. "All of it. That is why I care so much, you know. Why I have been so determined to fix this. After Father became sick and the stewards and men of business began squandering all of the family's fortunes, I should have known. I should have been paying more attention, spending more time at home. Then I would have realized that all was not right. But no, I was away at school, then spending time in London, having fun with my friends, playing a few pranks to release my boredom."

He waved his hand toward Devon, who looked as shocked as Cassandra.

"You cannot blame yourself for that," Devon said in a low voice. "You were doing what every young man of the *ton* does."

"That doesn't make it right," Gideon said. "If you don't mind, I will finish the rest of the accounts for the day before joining you for dinner."

"But—" Cassandra began, stepping forward, but Devon stopped her, gently placing his large hand over hers, lowering them down as he wrapped his other arm around her shoulders and began to steer her out the door.

"Let's leave Gideon be for a time, love."

"I'm not sure—"

"Go," Gideon said in a low voice as he sunk back into his chair. "Please."

As they walked out the door, arms around one another, Gideon had never felt so alone.

CHAPTER 2

"Well, little love, you don't mind me so much after all, do you now?" Madeline asked as she walked around the room with a soft bounce in her step, cradling the baby in her arms. The nanny had come a few times, offering to take him, but she had waved her away.

Madeline would never admit to anyone, not even Cassandra, how much she enjoyed having the warm bundle in her arms close against her, especially as he slept. She knew she should probably put him down in his cradle, but when he was snuggled up against her like this, his bottom high in the air, a peace settled into her soul that she had no intention of losing any time soon.

"He loves you."

Madeline looked up to find Cassandra standing in the doorway with a soft smile on her face as she whispered the words. Jack stirred at his mother's voice, and Madeline reluctantly passed him over.

He settled into Cassandra's arms but was soon bopping his head against her chest until Cassandra took a seat in the rocking chair and began to nurse him.

THE HEIR'S FORTUNE

Madeline had been surprised when Cassandra had announced her intention to feed her baby herself instead of hiring a wet nurse, but then, Cassandra never did anything that was expected of her.

"Thank you for spending time with us here at Castleton," Cassandra said softly as she stroked the baby's back. "I do appreciate having you here as we settle into life with Jack."

"I wouldn't want to be anywhere else," Madeline said with a smile, taking a seat in the other chair in front of the warm glow of the fire.

"What will you do after this?"

"After spending time with you here?"

"Yes," Cassandra said. "Eventually, I assume we will find the treasure – or find that it is not where it is supposed to be – and we will return home. Will you return to London for the Season?"

Madeline was silent for a moment. She had been trying not to think that far ahead.

"I am not sure of the point of returning to London," she said. "I have been out long enough that I have been introduced to every eligible young gentleman there is and none of them have any interest in me, my peculiar father, and my outspoken ways. Now that all of you are married… well, what would I do there? I'm not about to make friends with the young debutantes."

"You could."

Madeline snorted, covering her mouth with her hand when she saw Jack stir.

"I could, but you know how that would go."

"You would not put up with them."

"No, I wouldn't," Madeline admitted, shaking her head. "I am sure my father will insist on attempting again, however. He will be in London himself and I cannot stay alone in our country home. He has been optimistic that I will marry for five years now, and I think he actually still holds hope."

"Well, he should," Cassandra said. "I cannot understand why any man would *not* want to marry you."

"That's because you love me."

"I do."

"But you do not care how well off my family is, and as it happens, I have nearly as small of a dowry as one could imagine. Add that to my candid nature, and no gentlemen are knocking at my door for my hand."

"Not the right one," Cassandra said. "You know, it's funny... I was just having a conversation with Gideon about marriage."

Madeline heard the slight suggestion in her tone and lifted a brow at Cassandra.

"What are you trying to say?"

"Nothing at all. I was just noting the coincidence."

Madeline smirked. "If you are suggesting that Gideon and I should marry, then you should think again. Just because we are the only two left unmarried in our merry little bands does not mean that we belong together. I am the last woman who should ever be a duchess."

"Why would you say that?"

"Your family doesn't need any more scandal, and I would certainly bring some."

"Why? Because you are outspoken?"

Madeline didn't comment upon that for she didn't want to insult Cassandra's brother, but Gideon was far too staid a man for her to ever spend considerable time with. She would enjoy having some fun with him to see if she could break through that hard exterior, but that was the extent of it.

"Is something the matter?" Madeline asked, sensing there was more to this.

"Why would you ask that?"

Madeline shrugged. "You seem somewhat melancholy, even though you are doing a decently good job hiding it."

Cassandra laughed softly. "You always know what I'm thinking." She paused for a moment. "It's Gideon."

"His search for the treasure?"

"That is part of it, yes," she said. "He just holds the weight of all of Castleton on his shoulders. As though everything that happens here – that *has* happened to our family – is his fault, and he is willing to go to any lengths to set it right again. This treasure hunt… I have found it exciting, and fun, but what I have enjoyed most is that we have all done this together. He is the only one who is so completely focused on the end that he is not enjoying the journey."

"He is a serious man."

"Too serious. I suppose we can only hope that we find this treasure and it is what he has been waiting for."

"Or else?"

Cassandra sighed as she lifted the baby and held him against her chest, patting his back as she waited for him to burp.

"Or else I could be welcoming a sister-in-law that I'd rather not."

"What's that supposed to mean?" Madeline asked, confused.

"If we do not restore the family fortunes by finding a treasure, then Gideon will marry for a dowry that will allow us to do so."

"I see," Madeline said, uncertain why the thought made her so unsettled. It was a common enough occurrence – a dowry in exchange for a title of significance – but it didn't seem right that Gideon would have to do such a thing due to wrongs that were not his to start with.

Not that this had anything to do with her. She had her own future to worry about.

* * *

THE NEXT MORNING dawned bright but chilly as the autumn air began to settle in around Castleton. Madeline knew the staff kept the manor as warm as possible, but there were rooms that they left with empty hearths as they did all they could to save the money in the family's coffers.

It was admirable, though Madeline thought the Sutcliffes were a bit too fixated on rebuilding the dukedom. Madeline had been raised with a father who was indebted to a great number of men he had never been overly concerned with paying back and he didn't seem too particularly affected by it.

Cassandra and Devon had agreed to accompany Cassandra's mother, the duchess, that day as she visited families around their property and Jack was napping under the nanny's care, leaving Madeline a bit aimless – which, she supposed, was a reflection on her own life at the moment.

She wandered the manor for a time but found she was continually called in one direction – out of doors and toward the stables. It had been a couple of days since she had checked in on Lady, and she missed her.

Madeline told her maid of her plans and changed into her riding habit, and then slipped out before anyone saw her and insisted that she not go out of doors unaccompanied.

She was just leaving through the front entrance, however, when she found someone on her heels – someone unexpected, and much more welcome than any person might be.

"Look at you, little one," she said, reaching down and picking up the puppy, unable to stop herself from nuzzling his fur. "I am happy to see you have found a home in the house. Have they named you yet? No? Well, we just might have to do something about that."

She looked around to see if anyone was following them, but the hall behind her appeared to be empty.

"I am going to see my horse. You are more than welcome to come and meet her acquaintance, but you'll have to stay back in the stables while I ride, for you are too small yet to run beside us. What do you have to say about that?"

The dog cocked its head to the side as though in agreement before trotting along beside her as they meandered through the massive yet unmanicured gardens to the stables. At night, they would be the perfect setting for one of her Gothic novels.

Madeline greeted the one stablehand warmly, knowing how overworked he was. It had always surprised her that the few servants of Castleton were so loyal despite the amount of work required of them. Every time she visited, she recognized the same faces.

"How is Lady doing?" she asked Victor.

"Just fine," he said. "She has been here often enough that I think she feels right at home. She's been in the pasture this morning, but I can have her saddled for you shortly. Should I be preparing any other horses?"

"No thank you, Victor," Madeline said. "Just me."

"Should I ask a footman to—"

"No," she said, though with a smile to soften her words. "I should be fine."

"Very well," he said, nodding his head and ducking back into the stables. Soon enough he was leading Lady out toward her, and she accepted the reins from him.

"Lady Madeline, I should note—"

"Thank you, Victor," she said, not wanting to give him the opportunity to tell her that she should not be going out alone. She had enough of that from everyone else in her life – save her father. She didn't need it from the stablehand.

"Oh, if you could watch the puppy until I return, I would be ever so grateful."

He nodded, still appearing as though he wanted to say more, but he simply clucked his tongue toward the dog, who happily took off after him as Madeline pulled on her horse's reins and turned her away from the house and stables toward the open fields beyond Castleton. She had a fair understanding of where the Sutcliffe family's property began and ended. She and Cassandra had ridden together often enough before Cassandra had become with child.

Once Madeline knew she was out of sight of the house, she leaned down over her horse, urging her into a run. Nothing filled her with more joy than galloping, the closest sense to flying she knew she would ever experience. So often she looked up at the birds in the sky, wishing she had the same ability to freely go wherever she chose, without anyone or anything holding her back.

"That's it, Lady," she urged her on as the trees appeared in the distance. There was a lake beyond them where she might stop and rest for a time, although it wasn't the water that enticed her but rather stretch of trees that led there, which grew so close that their branches reached out to create dark, shadowy spaces to become lost in.

She was so focused she didn't hear the thundering of another horse's hooves until they were nearly beside her, the long, sleek black neck of the horse the first thing to enter her vision.

The second was the auburn hair of the tall figure of the man atop the horse. He was leaning forward, his form perfect, his natural speed faster than hers as he could ride astride and therefore had a better seat, although Madeline liked to think that her balance was far superior to any other woman and even most men.

But Lord Ashford was one of the best – he always had been.

As a young girl, Madeline had watched him riding away from Castleton through the large windows of the library, wishing that she could be out there as well, but she was too young to do so and would never have the ability without a proper chaperone.

Well, things were different now.

Most things, anyway.

It seemed Lord Ashford was as proficient as he had always been.

"Why are you alone?" he shouted through the wind rushing by them, and if she could have, she would have rolled her eyes. So predictable.

"I'll race you," she called back instead, pretending she hadn't heard his words.

"Race me?"

"To the trees," she said without giving him any time to turn her down. "Let's go!"

She urged Lady on faster, hoping that the few seconds of surprise would give her a chance to get ahead of him, which it did – for a moment.

Then he was gaining on her, and as much as she tried to deny it, there was no use – he was going to beat her.

The wind whipped through Madeline's hair as her riding cap must have flown off, but she had no care for it as the thundering hooves of the horses vibrated through her body.

The hoofbeats of Lord Ashford's horse were increasing, but she was not going to give up and let him win without a fight. She urged Lady on faster and faster until she was neck and neck with Lord Ashford's horse once more.

The two of them were so close that it seemed as though their horses were moving as one. She turned her head to look beside her, and for a moment, everything but the two of them and their horses faded away. All she could see was his deep blue eyes staring back at her, locked on hers as the world around them seemed to slow.

They were so close that she could have reached out and touched him, but then his horse surged forward, pulling ahead of hers, and all she could see was his powerful thighs gripping his stallion. Madeline urged Lady on, but it was no use. Lord Ashford was too far ahead and Lady had nothing left in her to catch him.

Breathless, they pulled their horses to a stop at the edge of the trees. Madeline patted Lady on the neck, nodding toward Lord Ashford despite how disheartened she was at the loss, her defeat annoying her when she was supposed to have been finding freedom.

Just when she didn't think that she could be more miserable, the first drop of rain hit her nose.

And then the skies opened up.

CHAPTER 3

"What are you doing out here alone?" he asked again as the rain fell upon them, soaking them through in seconds, and Madeline could only look at him incredulously.

"Are you so concerned about that right now? We have to return."

She was practically shouting to be heard, and he nodded grimly before turning his horse back toward the house. Their race had seemed short, but they had been riding fast and now their horses were wet and tired from their sprint, which made the return journey seem a lot longer and considerably more miserable.

They said nothing, Madeline turning inward as her riding habit and cloak were stuck to her skin in the most wretched way.

Suddenly Lord Ashford pushed his horse slightly ahead of hers before he stopped and dismounted, bending toward the ground. He walked over to her stopped horse and held his hand out toward her. Her mouth fell open in surprise when he held her crumpled, wet hat within it.

"You didn't have to," she said as loud as she could, shaking her head, but he simply shrugged his shoulders and remounted his horse, continuing on before she could recover from her surprise that he would take the time in the middle of a rainstorm to retrieve her hat.

They finally made it back to the stables, the relief of entering under a dry roof overcoming them, allowing Madeline to feel as though she could finally take a breath.

"How did the skies go from being empty to pouring rain?" she asked as she dismounted, looking around the stables but seeing only the few resident horses peering over their stalls at them. "And where is Victor?"

"Perhaps he was caught elsewhere when the rain began," Lord Ashford said, dismounting and beginning to see to his horse himself. Madeline followed suit, used to the task of looking after Lady. In fact, she rather enjoyed it.

"Had you wanted to spend time alone with me, Lord Ashford, you only had to ask," she teased, amused when panic crossed his face at her words.

"I thought I would be alone," he said tersely. "I spend most mornings riding around the property, overseeing everything. I had no idea that you would be riding as well."

"I am only jesting," she said, pushing her hair back away from her face. "Should we remove our riding clothes here?"

He stared at her as rain dripped from his hair, which had begun to curl around his head, and slid down his face.

"Are you still jesting?"

"Yes," she said, waiting a moment, and then she couldn't help it. She laughed out loud.

"Oh, Lord Ashford, you are a fun one."

"I am?" he said, his brow furrowed.

She guessed he had never been called that before. She didn't answer his question but instead began a different inquiry.

"You and your friends came together because you were a bored group of lords interested in undertaking some daring activities, did you not?"

"Yes," he said, removing his horse's saddle before crossing to hers. She had already unclasped it, but he waved her away when she tried to carry it.

"I have a hard time believing it."

He flicked a glance toward her. "Believe what you wish. It matters not to me."

"Allow me to rephrase," she said. "I suppose I wonder why you are a part of this circle of friends as you do not seem the type of man to participate in such dares or pranks?"

He was silent for over a minute as he continued to brush his horse, sluicing away the water that clung to its beautiful black sides.

"Do you remember me when I was younger?"

"Not entirely, as I was just a girl a few years younger than you myself," she said.

"I remember you."

"Do you now?" Well, this was interesting.

"You always had that harsh tongue of yours. You said the oddest things as a child, dressed in dark clothing that no other young ladies would ever be allowed to wear. You convinced Cassandra that ghosts were wandering the halls of Castleton."

"There probably are," she said, unable to understand how he couldn't give credence to the idea.

"As... unconventional as you were," he said, and Madeline started slightly, not liking his description, "you have always been sure of yourself and what you believed. I, however, was not at all."

She waited as she brushed her horse, knowing that a man like Lord Ashford needed the space to speak more than to be berated with questions.

"I was born to assume a title with no guidance from the man who should have been able to provide it," he said, not needing to explain his father, for Madeline was well aware that the duke was afflicted with an illness of the mind that left him coherent some days, stuck in the past on others, and often did not allow him to identify even those who were closest to him. "Yet the people who had been put in place to take care of everything ended up betraying us worse than anyone else."

"Those bastards," Madeline muttered, which earned her a sharp look from Gideon before his face dissolved into one of his rare smiles, as wry as it was.

"Bastards, yes," he said. "It left me uncertain of how I was to go about my life. Was I to assume the role of a child who would one day become a duke? Was I to make friends and go to school? Or was I to live as though I already held the responsibility?"

"No child should have to take on such a role," Madeline said quietly, but Gideon didn't seem to be listening to her any longer as he ran the brush over his horse absent-mindedly.

"I was lost. In my own shell. Not able to speak with others, hiding from both my family and my peers. Then a friend – a good friend, one I didn't deserve – went out of his way to bring me back to where I was supposed to be. Where I belonged."

"Lord Covington."

"Yes," he said with a nod. "Devon was the one who taught me what it meant to be my true self. I know I will never be as daring nor as outspoken as he, and that is completely fine. He spoke for me when I couldn't seem to find my voice. He advocated for me, and eventually, he was the one who brought us all together, if only to have a bit of fun. I couldn't say no to him."

"Do you regret it?"

"No," he said, shaking his head. "Not at all. These men have been the closest of friends as I could ever ask for and have been there for me in ways that I never thought possible. And they have shown me some fun that I would never have otherwise sought out myself. So no, I have no regrets."

"Not even now that they are all married, Lord Covington to your sister?"

He laughed humorlessly. "That did take some getting used to, especially when I learned about their past. But they are happy and that is all that matters."

"And you?" she said as she finished brushing Lady before seeing her back into her stall. "What will you do now?"

Why she was asking, she had no idea. Perhaps she had allowed her conversation with Cassandra earlier to get too much into her head.

"Now," he said, putting away all of the instruments he had used, carefully and meticulously, "I am going in to change."

* * *

THIS WAS EXACTLY why he tried to avoid this woman.

She asked questions that he had no desire to answer, and then once he started speaking to her, there was no stopping him. Why she wanted to know such things about him, he wasn't sure, but it was like she stored her secrets in some deep, dark vault, and any he got a taste of only left him wanting more.

Now their clothing was plastered to them, water running in rivulets from their hair, and he had spilled out some of his deepest thoughts in an effort to ignore the way that her blue riding habit formed to every curve in her body, showcasing her generous hips and bosom and her tight waist.

They were standing at the door of the stables now,

peering out toward the house, both of them wondering just when the rain might stop.

"I cannot see a rain this sudden keeping up for long," Gideon said as the house loomed so close, yet so far at the same time. He didn't have much desire to return to the elements, nor did he want to remain and answer Madeline's pressing questions. He had a feeling that she would have more to come. The woman was relentless.

"We are wet enough already," she said with a shrug. "What difference does it make?"

Without waiting for his response, she stepped out the doors, dashing toward the house as fast as she could.

Gideon cursed under his breath before he started forward, following her at a run as he untied his cloak. Once he reached her, he placed a hand on her arm, pulling her toward him as he lifted the cloak over her head.

"What are you doing?" she asked, turning her bright brown eyes toward him.

"Shielding you from the rain," he said, wondering why it wasn't obvious.

"I'm fine," she called back, although she made no move to remove his cloak, which told him that she had only been trying to be polite. The strange truth was that he rather liked looking after her, even in a small way.

The servant's entrance was closest to them, and they burst through the door, surprising a housemaid, who dropped a bucket which, thankfully, landed upright.

"My lord, my lady," she said, immediately dropping into a curtsy. "My apologies."

"Nothing to apologize for, Rose," Gideon said, waving a hand. "We were caught in the rain while riding. Continue as you were."

The girl nodded stiffly, bending to pick up her bucket. Just as they began to pass through the kitchens, a yap came from beyond, and the puppy Gideon had found came running toward them, jumping back and forth between Gideon and Madeline as though uncertain of just who was his master.

"What are you doing down here?" Gideon asked, bending to pat his head.

"My lord." Victor rounded the corner, relief on his face. "My apologies. I knew you were out in the rain and was concerned. I began to look for you, but then the dog ran out and I didn't want to leave him. Fortunately, he returned to the house."

The stablehand took a huge breath, and Gideon patted the dog absentmindedly.

"Had he come looking for me?" he asked.

"Er—that was actually my fault," Madeline said. "I let him accompany me to the stables and then asked Victor to watch over him. I didn't realize that anyone else was out riding – although I must apologize, Victor, for that is likely what you were trying to tell me."

Victor nodded once. "I should go see to the horses."

"We did that already," Gideon said. "It's still raining quite hard. Why do you not stay here, have yourself a hot drink, and then return once the rain has settled."

"That is kind of you, my lord," Victor said before Gideon and Madeline continued up the servants' staircase to the main part of the house.

"Have you named the dog?" Madeline asked.

"No," he said shortly.

"He needs a name."

"I know," Gideon said, trying to hide his annoyance.

"He's resilient and seems to be able to find his way, whether that is to people who need him or to find what he needs." She tapped a finger against her lip. "How about Scout?"

The dog gave a yap of excitement, causing Madeline to laugh.

"He agrees!"

"Well, Scout it is, then," Gideon said.

"Why did you not name him?"

"He's a dog."

"Lord Ashford," Madeline said boldly. "This dog already clearly adores you and as much as you are trying not to show it, you enjoy his company in turn. Would you like to know what I think?"

"Not really, but I have a feeling you are going to tell me anyway."

"I think that you do not want to allow the dog to get too close to you."

"Why would you think that?" he asked, turning away from her, for he did not like how close to the truth she was.

"You keep people – and dogs, apparently – at a distance."

"Because they all end up disappointing you," he said. "Now, this has been a pleasure Lady Madeline, but we should really both go find dry clothing."

"Scout, would you like to help us find the treasure?" Madeline said as they entered the dining room, their clothing dripping over the rich carpets as they went, but there was nothing to be done about it.

Gideon fixed her with a stare.

"Lady Madeline, there is no *us*. You will not be finding the treasure."

"What is that supposed to mean?"

"It is too dangerous. I cannot let you help."

She stopped, turning to him with her arms crossed over her chest. "I do not believe that you are in any position to tell me what to do."

"In this, I am."

"You are responsible for a lot of people, Gideon, but not for me."

"You are under my roof."

Her nostrils flared, but she said nothing. Instead, she turned around and strode away. It seemed he had finally said something that convinced her to leave him alone.

Except that Gideon had a feeling that wouldn't be the last of this conversation. Not at all.

CHAPTER 4

*M*adeline entered the dining room that night with purpose.

She hadn't allowed Lord Ashford to see how cold she was after their dousing of rain, but she had sat in a hot bath until the water grew cold and her fingers became wrinkled.

Now, she had donned an extra shawl for the evening, although no one seemed to question it.

In addition to Cassandra, her husband, and Lord Ashford, the duke and duchess attended dinner that evening, which Madeline welcomed.

They were a kind couple, one that truly loved one another. Their presence at dinner meant that the duke was having one of his better nights, although Madeline knew that he could still have moments of confusion.

"Good evening," Madeline said, taking a seat at the table with a flourish, smoothing out the satin of her navy skirts. She still preferred to wear dark clothing, opposing the style of the day, uncaring if she stood out from the other ladies.

"Good evening," they all said as one of Castleton's two footmen filled their glasses. Madeline steeled herself for the dinner to come. Castleton's cook left much to be desired. Madeline had no idea why they kept her on staff. They might not have a considerable amount of extra money, but surely they had enough to eat properly.

She supposed the loyalty went both ways.

"Turtle soup," a footman announced, and Madeline cringed, knowing from experience that the soup was certainly not turtle nor well made.

"Does anyone have any plans for tomorrow?" Madeline asked, looking around the table, trying not to catch Cassandra's eye, for their conspiracy might be too obvious. She had been sure to share with Cassandra her brother's ideas on who should be out looking for the treasure and Cassandra had the same opinion as Madeline about it.

"I think it's time that we begin our search," Gideon said, and Madeline had to hide her smile. He was falling right into her trap.

"Search for what?" his father asked.

"For the treasure, Father," Gideon said. He had told his father about this treasure hunt from the start, not hiding anything from him as Madeline knew he had asked his father for help with clues when necessary. Sometimes the duke had past experiences that had provided direction.

"Ah, yes," he said, although his eyes were far away.

"I am looking forward to it," Cassandra said with a bright smile. "We should start by using the necklace piece to determine where we are to go and then set out on our path."

Gideon cleared his throat. "First, I do not believe it is so simple. As you can imagine, I have spent a great amount of time looking at the map, and from what I can ascertain, it is not a straightforward path. I do not believe we can actually determine where we are to go until we are outside using the compass itself."

"Very good. We have a plan, then."

"We," Gideon held up a finger and waved it from him to Lord Covington and back again, "have a plan. Devon and I will go just the two of us. Perhaps we will ask a footman to join us in case we encounter any physical challenges."

Cassandra's mouth dropped open in shock. Considering that she had surmised his answer prior to this, Madeline was impressed with her acting.

This conversation was a reminder of not only how different Cassandra was from her brother but also why Madeline had been so unsuccessful in her campaign to find a husband. Her father had provided her more freedom than most and she would prefer not to have to succumb to the wishes of a man who might not be so lenient. Most of them were like Gideon with the expectation that the women in their lives would follow their wishes unquestioned.

"We have been with you from the start of this, Gideon," Cassandra said before she took a sip of her tea. "We will be there to see it through."

"You were with us before we knew that this hunt came with danger," he said, but then stopped when both of his parents looked up with concern.

"What sort of danger?" his mother asked, placing down her fork.

"The danger that comes from searching the paths of the grounds is all," Gideon said with a forced smile, and his mother nodded, although she looked unconvinced.

"Have the Spanish returned, then?" his father asked, taking a bite of his bread, which was, perhaps, the only edible food on their plates.

"Returned?" Gideon said, his eyebrows rising. As far as Madeline was aware, they hadn't shared with their parents that *Don* Rafael and his men had been so close to reaching Castleton after they had followed Faith and Lord Ferrington back to England. They had, however, been intercepted and seen to by the proper authorities.

"Yes, Grandfather chased them off not long ago when he found men on our land," the duke said, his reference to his grandfather indicating that he was having a momentary lapse back to the past. "He was worried they would return."

Gideon and Lord Ashford exchanged a glance.

"We'll keep an eye out," Gideon said.

Madeline knew that the threat that had followed them along this treasure hunt should leave her with some fear of what could be ahead if she stayed at Castleton, but she was more excited than anything about the risk. It wasn't that danger *appealed* to her, it was just that secrets and mysteries kept life interesting.

And not everything *had* to have a happy ending – a subject that she and Cassandra had argued more than once.

"Lady Madeline, how is your father?" the duchess asked, changing the subject.

"He is well," she said, before adding nonchalantly, "In fact, he is considering marrying again."

"Is he now?" The duchess asked, seemingly thrilled.

"Yes. He is concerned that he will be alone once I marry. I have told him that shouldn't be an issue, for I have no intention of that occurring anytime soon."

"Whyever not?" the duchess asked in surprise.

"Many reasons," Madeline said with a small, satisfied smile that she was, apparently, still unpredictable. "I suppose I have not yet found the right man."

"I'm sure you will one day, dear."

After dinner finished, instead of the gentlemen remaining in the dining room, the duchess suggested that they all make for the drawing room.

"Shall we play whist?" she asked, to which they agreed.

"We shall need partners. Cassandra, you and Lord

Covington best partner together. I will partner the duke, which leaves Gideon with Lady Madeline. Cassandra, why do you and Lord Covington not play Lady Madeline and Gideon first and then we shall play the victor?"

The duchess ushered them into places around the table, and Madeline found herself seated next to Gideon on the sofa, his hard thigh pressed against hers as she found she couldn't stay upright on the soft cushions of the sofa. It took all of the strength of her body to keep herself from falling into him.

Madeline was perturbed to discover, however, that she was not completely averse to their proximity. There was no denying that he was an attractive man and, at one time, perhaps she would have considered him a potential husband.

If she wasn't aware of how he had utterly betrayed Cassandra.

Cassandra might have forgiven Gideon and her mother for what they had done to her years ago. Madeline understood that they had thought they were in the right for sending her away when they had discovered her ruination, but it had affected Cassandra in ways that they couldn't imagine.

Madeline could not find it in herself to forgive them for it – nor forget.

No matter how much they might have thought they were doing the "right thing," ultimately, their love for their daughter and sister should have won out over whatever they thought society would expect.

At first, Madeline had hated Gideon for it. Over time, however, she had begun to understand the complexity of the situation. It lessened her degree of distaste for him, but she still could not imagine ever spending a great deal of time with a man who could do such a thing to his sister.

But here she was, his partner – for tonight, at least.

She glanced over at Gideon as he shuffled the deck of cards, his movements precise and controlled, as in everything he did. His blue eyes, so similar to Cassandra's and yet with a wariness that his sister did not possess, were intense and guarded when he met her gaze.

Madeline was never one to be uncertain as to what to say, and yet she found herself at a loss for words in the uncomfortable silence of the room.

For quite some time she had wanted to confront him about the decision he had made in the past, but Cassandra had asked her to let it go and move on as she had, telling her that all had ended well and to bring it up again would only be causing trouble where it was no longer found.

At the moment, Cassandra and her husband were so involved with one another that they hardly seemed to recognize anyone around them. Perhaps once one found such a great love, nothing else much mattered anymore.

In the end, it was Gideon who spoke first. "You are very quiet tonight, Lady Madeline. Is something troubling you?"

Madeline was taken aback by his question for she had not expected him to be attentive nor to inquire as to her feelings even if he had noticed, but she quickly composed herself and responded simply with, "No. I am quite well, thank you. Shall we begin?"

At Gideon's nod of agreement, they began to play against Cassandra and Lord Covington. Madeline was not surprised to find that Gideon's skills in the game were quite adept. While he was not the type of man to spend a great deal of time gambling, he was observant and quick-thinking, so she could at least take comfort that he would be a capable partner for the game. Madeline had learned whist from her father, as she had most card games, for he enjoyed gambling more than anything else in the world. She wasn't sure how much Gideon knew about that, however.

It quickly became evident that the two sides were well matched, each one successfully thwarting the other's designs until it was time for them to draw their hands for the last round.

As they did so, Gideon tensed beside her, and she could not help but sense a certain level of tension between them as they tried to outwit each other. While they had been acquainted for nearly her entire life, never before had she found herself in such an intimate setting with him, especially one which required them to not only interact but to do so in such proximity. His presence was strangely soothing yet thrilling.

The game came down to a single trick, and when Gideon threw down his final card, Madeline's heart raced as she waited for the outcome – who would be victorious?

In the end, it was Cassandra and Lord Covington, and Madeline groaned aloud as she threw back her head.

When she returned upright, Cassandra was laughing, while Gideon and his mother looked rather ill-at-ease, and Madeline realized that she had been rather overzealous.

She cleared her throat and stood, relinquishing her seat at the card table.

"My apologies," she said, stepping backward. "That was well played."

"There is absolutely nothing to apologize for," Cassandra said, shaking her head. "Mother and Father, I believe you will face us now."

Gideon traded seats with his father, but Madeline decided that she'd had enough of cards for one evening. She appreciated how much this family accepted her, but the more time she spent with them, the more she was reminded that she was still an outsider and alone in the world but for a father who wanted to be rid of her.

"I believe I am going to say goodnight," she said, prepared

to leave when the duke raised his head and looked at her, his eyes clear and piercing.

"You remind me of my grandmother."

"Your grandmother?" she repeated in surprise, uncertain of whether or not she should be glad of the comparison.

"Yes," he said. "She was daring and outspoken and my grandfather loved her dearly."

With that, he took the seat his son had vacated and began to shuffle the cards methodically – in very much the same way as Gideon himself.

Madeline took a step back, the evening reminding her that while Cassandra was her good friend, Madeline was not a true part of this family.

Nor any family, truly. All she had was a father who saw her as a burden and would prefer that someone else look after her.

She knew she would have to marry eventually – she didn't have many other options – but she had given up on finding love.

Her friends were happy, yes.

She just had to come to accept that it would not be the same fairy tale story for her.

CHAPTER 5

Madeline didn't sleep well that night, which wasn't unusual. She often went to bed far later than anyone else, wandering the halls and speaking to the ghosts who accompanied her.

She liked the dark, the silence that awaited, and if she truly couldn't sleep, she would visit the library until she found a book that would lull her to dreams – which meant that her true favorites, the gothic novels, would have to wait until later in the day, for they would surely mean that she would be up all night until she finished them.

When her maid entered and threw back the thick crimson curtain, Madeline buried her head under her pillow, trying to tell the girl to leave her be, until she remembered – today was the day.

The day they were going to find the treasure.

Well, attempt to find it. She wasn't completely optimistic about their chances.

She and Cassandra had devised a plan. While the men thought that they would be searching for the treasure on their own, Madeline and Cassandra were going to be following behind. They deserved to be present for the discovery as much as the men did.

They had both decided to dress in dark green so that they would blend in with their surroundings and when they met at the breakfast table along with the men, Cassandra refused to meet her eye. Madeline knew it was because she was worried that in doing so, she would give them away. They had come too far for that.

"Be sure to eat enough for your great search today," Cassandra said to her husband as she spread jam over her toast. "You should not want to have to cut it short for a luncheon."

Her husband snorted. "I should think not." He paused, staring at her more carefully. "You know that the only reason you are not coming with us is because of the danger."

"I do not believe there is any danger remaining as *Don* Rafael and his men were captured," Cassandra said. "But so be it."

Lord Covington looked at her suspiciously but didn't say anything, and when Cassandra waved him away after he placed a kiss on her cheek, he wore such a smitten expression that it seemed she had distracted him from the truth.

"You practically told him what we were doing!" Madeline accused her a short time later as they quickly donned their hats and cloaks before beginning their tail.

"I did nothing of the sort!" Cassandra countered.

"Oh, darling, be sure to eat," Madeline said in a high, mocking voice as she swooned back and forth, fluttering her eyes. Cassandra swatted her but started to laugh.

"I do not sound like that!"

"You do, in a way."

"I am a woman in love. I cannot help myself. Someday, you shall understand."

Madeline looked down at her hands as she pulled on her

black leather gloves and they started down Castleton's wide staircase. "I am sure that if I marry, it will not be for love."

"Why would you say that?" Cassandra asked, hurrying to keep up with Madeline's long strides.

"Because it would have happened by now," Madeline said. "But enough of that. We must keep our wits about us."

"Should we tell anyone where we are going?" Cassandra asked, looking around her, and Madeline shook her head.

"Of course not. Anyone we tell would feel obligated to inform your brother."

"You're right," Cassandra said, setting her jaw with a firm nod of her head. "I am not trying to be foolish. If we were anywhere else, I would never go alone. But these are the grounds of Castleton. I grew up here, running around the gardens and paths as a child. If the men leave our property, then we will not follow, but if they remain here, I do not see any problem in us being part of this."

Madeline smiled, lifting her head. "I like how you think."

"Of course you do. That is why we are such good friends."

They linked arms and began down the path, keeping Gideon and Lord Covington in their sights ahead. The men did not carry the map, as they had studied it back at the house and then written out directions as to where they thought they should go. They were worried about bringing the map along with them, in case they were to lose it or damage it along the way. They had decided they would return for a footman if necessary, which worked to the ladies' advantage for it was one less person who might notice them.

"Do you think they read the map properly?" Madeline asked suspiciously.

"They are both intelligent men."

"Are they, though?" Madeline asked, raising a brow, and

Cassandra suddenly grabbed her arm and pulled her behind a rather rotund statue.

"Did they see us?" Madeline asked.

"No, but they were looking back this way."

"Are they lost?"

"I don't know!" Cassandra said, laughing. "I would tell you if I thought we should worry. But no, they seem to know where they were going."

Madeline popped her head back up over the rock.

"They're moving again," she said, tugging Cassandra up behind her, turning around when she saw that Cassandra hadn't moved.

"What is it?" Madeline asked impatiently. "We must go."

"I need to ask you something."

"Very well, but you should probably be quick about it."

"Why do you hate my brother?"

Madeline started, jolting backward.

"Do we need to talk about this now?" she asked, and Cassandra nodded.

"Before we find this treasure. It's important. You're my best friend and he's my brother and I always feel that there's this tension there between the two of you."

Madeline sighed and waved her hand. "Very well. But I'll be quick. I do not hate your brother. But I also do not trust him. Not after what he did to you."

"That is in the past, Madeline," she said with exasperation. "I have told you that. All has worked out as it should."

"You are a better person than I am, Cassandra."

Cassandra stood. "You know that is not true. We should continue, but I do ask you to promise me this – do not hold this against Gideon anymore. Not for me. He's a good person, and he's changed. I want us to find this treasure as a unified group."

"While we are following behind at a distance?" Madeline asked, lifting an eyebrow.

She looked up at the retreating backs of the men, worried that they were going to lose them, but before she could do so, they heard a cry echoing through a window from the house – the cry of a baby.

Cassandra looked up at the high window of the nursery with despair, obviously torn between soothing her baby and continuing their quest, but Madeline waved toward the house.

"Go."

"I do not want to leave you."

"I know, but your baby needs you. I'll follow the men and leave clues along the way so you can follow." She spied the rowan tree beside them and inspired, snapped a branch off. "I'll scatter the rowan berries along the path."

"Very well," Cassandra said. "You best go – hurry!"

Madeline nodded, squeezing Cassandra's arm before lifting her skirts and taking off down the path after the men, who had disappeared from her vision. They were headed over the rise, toward the road beyond which would lead them through the ruins and closer to the treed area of the property. From listening to Gideon and Lord Covington as they reviewed the map, she knew that they had determined their starting point, and from there, they would use the compass to follow the route.

She was so forward-focused while keeping up her pace, dropping berries, and not making too much noise, that she wasn't as in tune with the surroundings behind her as she should have been.

Which was why she didn't see them until it was too late.

A hand slapped over her mouth, her arms were pinned behind her back, and she was lifted off the ground without warning.

And no matter how hard she tried, she had no chance of fighting back.

* * *

Gideon's heart was racing.

Today could be the day that all he had been working toward for the past few years could come true.

"Thank you for doing this with me," he said to Devon, who looked at him with surprise as he strolled down the path with that carefree way of his, hands in his pockets, lips pursed as he quietly whistled.

"Of course. Our companion appears to be equally pleased to accompany us."

They looked down at Scout, who was trotting along beside them as though he knew exactly where he was going and how important this mission was. He looked backward every now and then as though searching for something — or someone — but Gideon couldn't see anyone nearby.

"Here we are," Gideon said as they neared the end of the cleared walking path, "the edge of the property, where the path meets the woods."

He pulled the compass out of his pocket, holding it out in front of him.

"I believe we are to travel due north."

Devon nodded, his jaw ticking, the only sign as to how much he was also anticipating what they might find.

"How upset was Cassandra?" Gideon asked as they continued single file on what was now a path that had been created by multiple foot treads. Besides their voices, the only sound around them in the crisp autumn air was their feet in the dry leaves beneath them and the dog panting beside them.

"Actually," Devon said, tilting his head in contemplation, "she was not nearly as irritated as I thought she might be."

Gideon looked toward him. "Should we be concerned?"

Devon sighed, but there was a smile on his face. "Likely."

Gideon was, not for the first time, grateful that a man like Devon was the one who had married his sister despite his initial reservations. There weren't a lot of men who would have not only allowed her to be her true self but would actually love her for it.

She had no care for the conventions of the era – much like Madeline, he contemplated, although why he would think of her, he had no idea.

"What do you think the treasure will be?" he asked Devon, finally allowing himself to consider the outcome, but before Devon could answer, Scout abruptly stopped, his ears standing straight up and back on his head as he turned around to look behind them on alert.

"What's wrong, boy?" Gideon asked.

"A squirrel or rabbit?" Devon suggested.

Before they could determine what had captured his attention, however, Scout took off back the way they had come, barking as though he was on attack.

"Scout!" Gideon called after him. "Come back!"

He looked at the path they had been following with regret, but as much as he hadn't wanted to allow himself any attachment to this dog, he had no wish to lose him. He had begun to like having the little guy around and he started behind him at a quick pace.

"We'll see what's bothering him and then return," Gideon called over his shoulder to Devon as they broke out of the trees into the sunlight.

Scout was already out of sight over the rise before them, but they could still hear him, his barks only becoming angrier. Gideon and Devon pushed themselves to the top of the incline, breathing heavily as they stopped and looked out over the landscape before them.

The scene that awaited him had Gideon's heart pounding. Four men on horseback stood below them in a defensive semicircle. But that wasn't what had Gideon so upset. It was why the fifth horse was without a rider.

For the rider was standing on the ground, a woman in front of him. Her cloak covered her dark green dress, her nearly black hair glinting in the sunlight while her hat lay on the ground at her feet.

And a pistol was leveled at her head.

"My God," Devon said under his breath beside him as they watched Scout bark in anger as he dove toward them.

Unlike any other time in his life, Gideon didn't stop to think – instead he sprang into action, allowing his legs to churn under him as he took off after the dog. He assumed Devon was behind him, and he remembered that he had brought his weapons – but they would be useless when it was only the two of them against this number of men.

The only thought that flew through his mind as he ran down the hill was that he could not allow anything to happen to Madeline, no matter how helpless he felt.

Not now.

Not ever.

CHAPTER 6

Madeline closed her eyes and tried to breathe after she let out a gasp when she realized that she had been holding her breath.

"Who are you?" she demanded again, but the men said nothing, only holding her tightly as they waited – for what, she wasn't entirely sure.

Then she heard Scout's bark and a tear leaked out of her eye, although she wasn't sure whether it was in relief or despair that it could put him in danger – as well as the men he was with.

Men that, despite how much they aggravated her at times, meant something to her as well.

"Call off your dog!" One of the men on horseback shouted in heavily accented Spanish, and Madeline drew in a breath. Were they back? The same men who had attacked Faith and Eric? "If you do not stop him, I will shoot him!"

Madeline had to clamp her lips shut to keep from calling out or sobbing, but she refused to give them any satisfaction.

"Scout, back!" Gideon called out, enough desperation in

his tone that the untrained dog understood enough to stop. Although what that meant for her, Madeline had no idea.

There were plenty of damsels in distress in her gothic novels, but Madeline had never had any desire to be one of them.

She had always thought that if she were to relate to any character in her stories, it would be the villainess who had tempted the chaste hero away from his noble goal.

But, alas, here she was.

How disappointing.

Gideon came to a stop in front of them, his spine straight and his hands fisted at his sides. He was a rather lean man, and could often be lost in a crowd, especially if he was beside a large man like Lord Ferrington or someone much more debonair such as Lord Covington.

But right now, Gideon had summoned all of the ducal power within him and was standing tall as he stared at the men who surrounded them. When his eyes landed on the man who held Madeline, a shiver worked its way down her spine due to the cold, steely determination in his stare.

He was furious.

She had never seen this side of Gideon before. He was reserved. Regal. Respectful, his emotions under tight control.

All of that had been stripped away, leaving bare emotion in its place.

And, despite her current situation and the very real danger they were facing, Madeline was suddenly captivated.

"Release her," he said, his voice dropping an octave with the grit that filled it.

"And just why," the man said, "would I do that?"

"You are on British soil," Gideon continued as Devon stood only a foot behind him. "On *my* land. The land of a duke. You are holding a woman who is currently under my protection. You must understand that there is no optimal end to this scenario for you."

"You have many words, but we have many weapons," the man said with a smirk. "Not to worry. I will return her to you. But it will come with a price – the map."

"Map?" Gideon said, but, unfortunately, he was not the most skilled liar. "What map?"

"The map you stole from *Don* Rafael," one of the other men said.

"No one *stole* anything," Gideon said. "If anything was taken, it was something that was ours to begin with."

Madeline held her breath again as the man beside her pressed the pistol harder into her temple.

"Your sister's death would mean nothing to us," he seethed. "It wouldn't be the first time that I have killed."

Even as her stomach started to twist, Madeline didn't miss exactly what he said. Sister?

They thought she was Cassandra.

That could be cause for great relief, or also great fear.

They would likely think that killing Cassandra would have greater consequences – but worse, if they realized she *wasn't* Cassandra, there was a good chance they would go looking for her in truth.

Madeline could not allow that to happen.

She had no death wish, but Cassandra was a mother and Madeline had to make sure that she stayed safe.

She looked Gideon in the eye, shaking her head as imperceptibly as she could to signal to him not to reveal her true identity.

Was she imagining it, or did he slightly nod in return?

"Very well," Gideon said, although his face trembled with his anger. "You can have the map. But I do not have it with me."

"Then go fetch it and bring it to us. One of my men will

go with you to ensure you do not call for help," the man commanded, but Gideon shook his head.

"I will not leave my… sister here alone with you."

"Your friend can stay. The map – now."

Gideon looked from Madeline back to Lord Covington.

"Do you have her?" he asked Lord Covington in a tone low enough that he sounded like a different man.

"Of course," Lord Covington said, and when his hands kept twitching toward his waistband, Madeline knew he had weapons hiding that he was sorely tempted to use. She wished he wouldn't, for she had a pretty good idea that it wouldn't end well – for any of them.

Gideon turned back to Madeline's captors. "How do I know that we will stay safe after we give you the map?"

"I suppose you will just have to trust us."

Madeline didn't need to see the man's face to know that was the last thing they should do.

At least Gideon was smart enough to realize the same.

"I need reassurance."

"What do you propose?" the Spaniard asked, but before Gideon could respond, a shot resounded from beyond – and as they all paused in shock, one of the men suddenly teetered and then slid off of the horse, until he was hanging limply by the stirrups.

All hell broke loose.

The Spaniards began yelling at one another as the two flanking the outside began riding wildly from side to side as they searched for the source of the gunshots. As they did so, more shots rang out, and Madeline crouched low, wishing she could, at least, cover her head with her arms, although what good that would do, she had no idea.

"Madeline!" she heard Gideon call out as he inched forward toward her, Devon behind him with his own pistol drawn, but Madeline's captor was holding her as a shield.

She locked eyes with Gideon, a deep connection drawing them together, and his blue eyes seemed to be staring right through her soul, speaking to her, telling her that, some way, he would get them through this and out the other side. Despite the chaos around them, a strange sense of peace washed over her.

Madeline was far from the most optimistic person in the world. She always thought it was best to believe the worst and then be pleasantly surprised if anything better came along.

But now, before her, was Gideon. He kept coming closer, slowly but surely moving forward despite all the chaos that surrounded them. In those few seconds, Madeline trusted him completely. Deep down she knew that no matter what happened here today, Gideon would do whatever it took to make sure she got out alive.

Except it wouldn't happen at that exact moment.

For just when she thought that he would come close enough to save her, the strong arms behind her circled her waist, picked her up, and threw her over the horse.

The Spaniards were retreating – and they were taking Madeline with them.

* * *

"Madeline!"

Gideon raced after them, running as hard as he could, trying with everything within him to catch the horses as they took off away from them, no matter how futile he knew the effort was.

At some point in the pandemonium, one of the Spaniards had cut loose the dead man, and the fifth horse followed along behind them. Gideon chased after it, trying to grab the reins so that he would have a chance at catching the others,

THE HEIR'S FORTUNE

but it broke away and Gideon soon found his arms flailing wildly.

"Fuuuck!" he yelled out as finally his lungs and legs could no longer keep up their pace.

"Gideon."

Devon's voice behind him, his breathing just as ragged, called to him to stop, but Gideon did not want to give up now.

"Gideon, stop."

Devon's large hand came to rest on his shoulder, drawing him back.

"They're gone," he said. "We have no chance to catch them."

Gideon turned to Devon, pushing him away, even though he knew that he had no issue with his friend but was only taking his frustrations out on the closest person. He had to call Scout back a few times until the dog finally stopped chasing and barking and returned to him, his head hanging low in defeat.

"They *took* her," Gideon said slowly before the panic resounded in his voice. "They took her! What are we supposed to do? She was under our care. What the hell are they going to do with her? They are—"

"Stop," Devon said, more firmly this time. "There is nothing we can do right now, not when we are on foot. We will go back to the house and decide what to do from there."

Gideon nodded, his jaw tense and tight, as they started back toward the estate as quickly as they could.

"Why did you shoot the one rider?" he asked, trying to tell himself that Devon was only doing what he thought was best and not to blame him for initiating the shootout that had led to the men leaving with Madeline.

"I didn't shoot anyone," Devon said, looking over at him

in confusion as they reached the gardens. "I have no idea where that shot came from."

"It wasn't you?" Gideon said, his eyebrows drawing together. "Then who else was out there?"

"I have no idea," Devon said grimly. "But I am beginning to feel that there is someone around here who knows a lot more than they are letting on."

"And are either helping or hindering – it is hard to say," Gideon said as they drew closer to the house. "What am I supposed to tell Cassandra?" he asked, rubbing a hand over his face. "She is going to be livid."

"She'll probably be more worried than anything, no matter how she reacts," Devon said. "Pay no mind to whatever she says to you. She'll just be lashing out. Similar to someone else I know."

"But—"

He hadn't been able to finish the sentence as the front doors flew open and Cassandra came running out. "There you are!" she said. "I was looking everywhere. I followed Madeline's berries until suddenly they stopped and you were nowhere to be found afterward. Then I heard gunshots, but of course, so did Mother, and she refused to allow me to come look for you. I only listened to her because I would never want to leave Jack."

She looked at the two of them, then around more wildly, panic beginning to build judging by the tension in her face and the flapping of her arms. "Where's Madeline?"

Gideon took a breath, stealing a look over at Devon for courage, remembering that his friend was there for additional support, for both him and Cassandra.

"She's—" he started, pausing for a moment.

"She is gone. Captured by the Spanish men who stole onto our property," Devon finished for him, and Gideon couldn't help his annoyance that his friend would think him incapable of sharing the news.

"You cannot be serious," Cassandra said, but her mouth was still shaped in a round O, her eyes wide and searching as she knew they were telling the truth but didn't want to accept it. "I saw her but minutes ago. I was following her. I was—"

Devon was immediately at her side, placing his arm around her and pulling her in close. "I know."

Cassandra looked up at him, her eyes beginning to water. "This is all my fault. You said it was too dangerous, Gideon, but we wanted to come anyway. And then I left her alone when the baby cried and now she has been taken away from us. If I hadn't asked her to come to Castleton—"

"It is not your fault," Gideon said harshly, even as he knew he could never share the fact that the captors had thought that Madeline was Cassandra. His sister's guilt would be too heavy. "It was mine. She was at my home, under my protection. I should have known that the two of you would never do as you were told. Even more so, I never should have let her stay here in the first place."

"We are not children," Cassandra snapped.

"What is it with the two of you and your insistence on placing blame?" Devon asked in exasperation, cutting through their tension. "None of that is going to help. If you must blame someone, blame the people who took her."

"You're right," Cassandra said leaning into him. "And even more importantly, you have to go after her – before... before..."

She couldn't say it, but Gideon knew exactly what she meant – before it was too late.

CHAPTER 7

Madeline wished she spoke better Spanish.

It should not be her most pressing concern at this moment, but she had never been one given to hysterics. She had no choice now but to try to extricate herself from this situation, for she didn't think there was much chance that anyone else would be doing so.

Would anyone come after her? She supposed they would try – Gideon would feel they had to, out of duty if nothing else. But with Gideon and Devon on foot and she on horseback with her captors, there was little chance of them ever discovering just where they had taken her.

She didn't have much idea herself.

After they had fled Castleton, they had come to a stop and lifted her onto the riderless horse.

She had considered urging the horse on to try to escape, but her captors had made it abundantly clear that they would have no qualms about killing her if it came to that. Seeing as how they each carried a pistol and one was aimed at her head the entire time, she wasn't about to take the chance.

Would Gideon come for her, or would it be Lord Covington? She wasn't sure that Lord Covington would ever actually leave Cassandra and the baby, but it was equally difficult to picture Gideon riding to her rescue.

He wasn't much of a white knight. Perhaps a grey one – sullen, only there out of duty and not because of his need to be the hero.

They hadn't travelled particularly far, and best she could tell, they were in some kind of cabin deep in the woods on a property nearby.

It exuded an eerie stillness, as though it had been frozen in time. When they had arrived that afternoon, dust particles were dancing in the faint rays of sunlight filtering through the tattered curtain, while faded paper adorned the walls.

She hoped that someone would see that this abandoned cabin was abandoned no longer and word would reach Castleton.

Madeline looked around the small room they had put her in. Her hands were tied behind her, attached to a bedpost. They hadn't even allowed her to sit on the bed, but rather on the dusty floor. They had given her some sips of water, but so far nothing to eat. She wondered what kind of captors they would be, and for the first time, her heart started pounding in fear of just what might exactly happen to her.

The Spaniards were bickering at the moment, and from the few words she could pick up in their conversation, they were trying to decide just what they were to do with her, and how they could still use her to get what they wanted.

The map was a piece of it, but there was more to it, and it seemed the only way they knew out of this was still to trade her for what they were waiting for.

"Senorita," one of the men called before gesturing her into the room with them, and a sick sense of dread began to fill her stomach. She said nothing until finally one of them realized she was still bound and came in to untie her from the bed. This man appeared to be the most junior of the group, and there was more compassion in his eyes than the others. Perhaps Madeline could convince him to set her free if she ever was able to speak to him alone.

Her steps were heavy, causing the weathered and creaky wooden floorboards to groan as the man tugged her into the main room, stopping when all eyes turned toward her.

They were huddled around the remnants of a stone fireplace, having made a small fire in the hearth. Madeline dearly wished that she could capture some of its warmth.

This would be the type of place she would love to explore, to discover what it would whisper to her about the bygone era and the remnants of forgotten life that still lingered in the air, telling tales of days when the room was alive with the warmth of human presence. These men were marring those memories, and Madeline was annoyed by it almost as much as she was upset that she had to be here with them.

"Write," one of the men said, gesturing to paper and pen on a long, dilapidated table that sat in the middle of the room. Its surface was damaged by scratches and stains, a discarded, moth-eaten rug at her feet, its once-vibrant patterns now faded and indistinct.

She slowly took a seat on the solitary, dust-covered chair in front of the table, picking up the pen they had left for her before looking down at the rest of them. She pushed a frayed lace doily, yellowed with age, out of the way.

"Well?" she said. "What would you like me to say?"

* * *

"I've said farewell to Cassandra and Jack. I'm ready when you are."

Gideon turned from his horse's side to look at Devon,

who stood in the doorway of the stable. "You are not coming with me."

Devon crossed his arms over his chest.

"Last I checked, I was a grown man. An earl at that. Seems I can do as I wish."

Gideon was already shaking his head as he saddled up his horse.

"When you married my sister, you promised me that you would always look after her, and whatever children might come. Now she is here, alone, and in need of you. You are not coming because you have responsibilities that are far more important than mine."

"That's low, using my family like that."

"It's the truth," Gideon said, walking out of the stable alongside Devon. "Not only that but what if somehow the Spaniards return? We cannot leave them here without anyone to watch over them."

"There are our mystery protectors."

"That we have no idea who they are or what they would want."

"How are you going to take on four men alone?" Devon asked, although he was already pulling the pistols out and passing them to Gideon.

"I'm not," Gideon said. "I will find Madeline and try to extricate her without them noticing."

"How will you find her?"

Gideon sighed, lifting his head to meet Devon's eyes, in which they shared the truth with one another, a truth that neither of them wanted to say aloud.

"That I do not know," Gideon said quietly, but he was soon cut off by the sound of a voice ringing through the air.

"Lord Ashford! Lord Ashford!"

They exchanged a glance before rushing from the stables

just in time to see a man on horseback thundering down the entry road toward them.

He came to a stop ahead of them, lifting his hands from the reins and holding them in a show of peace.

"You are one of them!" Gideon said, beginning to charge toward him. "Where is she?"

"Whoa," the man said, as though Gideon was a horse. "Message."

He held the paper out toward Gideon, who would have loved to rip the man off the horse and beat him until he revealed all, but he could hardly attack an unarmed man.

"What does it say?" Devon asked, as he came to stand and read over Devon's shoulder while keeping one careful eye on the messenger.

"Brother. I am fine, as of now. The men have not hurt me. They will return me to you in exchange for the map, or the treasure if you have found it. They ask us to meet at the abandoned mill tomorrow at noon."

Gideon lifted his head to glare at the man. "Where is she?"

The man shrugged his shoulders before flashing a grin at him, and Gideon would have loved to wipe that grin off his face, but Devon leaned in and spoke lowly in his ear.

"Killing him will accomplish nothing."

Gideon nodded slowly, a plan forming in his mind.

"Go tell your friends. We will see you tomorrow."

The man nodded before turning his horse around and taking off. Gideon turned to Devon.

"Are you thinking the same thing I am?" he said.

"That your horse is saddled and ready and this man is headed to meet the rest of his friends and likely Madeline? Yes. Go."

Gideon was already running to the stables when Devon called out to him again.

THE HEIR'S FORTUNE

"Don't do anything stupid. If you cannot escape with her, then we have another place we can meet them tomorrow."

Gideon nodded, agreeing.

He had to be smart about this. As he swung himself upon his horse, Knightly, he reminded himself that he was Lord Ashford, future duke. He had repaired all manner of things, from relationships to accounts to debts paid.

Surely he could save one woman from a pack of thieves.

He kept the messenger just within his line of sight as he tracked him through the land that he knew better than anyone, having spent his youth riding its paths and his adult life caring for them.

It was then he realized that since Madeline's disappearance, he had not once considered the treasure or the possibility of having to give it up.

For, if it came to that – he would, he considered with dawning realization.

No treasure was worth more than a person's life, especially when that person was such close friends with his sister.

That was the only reason. He was sure of it.

The messenger didn't travel far, thank goodness, for Gideon was not prepared for an overnight journey. Gideon realized exactly where he was going as he neared the abandoned cabin, just a couple hours' ride from Castleton. At one point in time, it had been a dwelling for one of the tenants, but no one had lived there for years, not since they had parceled the land. He wondered if these men had planned to use it or had simply gotten lucky and stumbled upon it.

Either way, he had explored it years ago, so he knew where the bedroom was located and where he guessed they would be trying to keep warm around the fireplace – that is, if there was anything left of it. The stone had been near to crumbling the last he had seen it.

The darkness had set in as he was riding, and there was a

slight enough glow through the grimy glass panes of the front windows to tell him that they had been able to start a fire.

Gideon tied his horse to a tree a fair distance away so that he wouldn't make any noise and signal his arrival before creeping toward the house as quietly as he could. He drew one of the pistols out, holding it in front of him in case any surprises awaited, but from what he could tell, they hadn't expected company.

The captors' horses were tied to a long post at the side of the yard, but besides one soulful whinny, they didn't make much note of him.

Gideon rounded the side of the house, trying to remember just where the bedroom might be – he'd start there and, if he had to, wait until the men were sleeping before attempting any rescue.

Keeping close to the house, he found the window and inched upward until he could peer within. It was grimy, the curtains to the side laced with cobwebs, and so dark that it was difficult to see anything, except – there. His heart nearly stopped beating in his chest when he saw movement on the floor.

Those bastards hadn't even allowed her the decency of sitting on a piece of furniture, as dusty and old and uncomfortable as it might be. The ire began to bubble up within him, but there was another emotion accompanying it – one that took him off guard.

It was the desperation to rescue her, to be sure that she came to no harm – and an overwhelming fierce need to protect her. He prayed she was currently in the same state that she had left Castleton.

When Madeline had been held captive on his land, her hands behind her back, pistol at her head, there had been fear on her face then, yes, but that was not all. There was also an intense air of defiance in the way that she held herself, refusing to give in to whatever it was these men wanted from her. He admired that about her, as much as it equally worried him.

He didn't know Madeline particularly well, but what he did know of her was that she didn't fear much – in fact, he would prefer that she feared *more*. Perhaps then, they would not be in this current predicament.

Gideon nearly broke through the window right then, until voices resonated from the room beyond, floating through the thin walls and cracked window. He closed his eyes, able to discern at least two different men who were arguing in Spanish. Perhaps these were the leaders.

Gideon could not speak Spanish as well as he would like, but he knew enough of similar languages to determine that they were trying to decide their course of action when they met him the next day – whether they would kill them all and take the map, or use them to find the treasure and *then* do away with them.

He swallowed hard, the urgency of this rescue becoming much more certain. They couldn't wait for tomorrow's meeting. It would be far too risky.

He had to act now.

CHAPTER 8

Gideon had dressed in his warmest wool clothing, and yet, the cold dampness of the autumn air seemed to sink right through his skin as he waited outside the window. Night was blanketing the house, and he wondered whether he should wait for the men to fall asleep, or to try to free Madeline while the men were still arguing.

He paused, closing his eyes to try to picture what the cabin looked like. From what he could remember, there was only one bedroom. And no matter what arrangements the men might have made, the idea of a warm bed with a woman nearby might be too tempting. He couldn't risk waiting.

He studied the window more closely. It was a casement window, likely opening with a latch from inside.

But it had also been constructed many years ago, and the wood had decayed. He was sure he could easily open it; the question was how much noise he would make while doing so.

Gideon found his pocketknife and opened it to the longest blade. He slid it along the wood that housed the windowpanes, breaking the board off from its casing. A small crack sounded, causing movement within, and he hoped it was only Madeline. He continued, praying the rest of his efforts would remain silent until he finally had enough broken free. He was just about ready to try to break the window off when it swung open from the inside and he fell backward in surprise, landing on his buttocks in the damp brush below.

"Lord Ashford?" came the hushed, surprised voice, and he looked up to see Madeline hanging from the window above. Her hair was dishevelled and her face was dirty but otherwise, she appeared to be relatively unharmed. "You came."

"Of course, I came," he said, trying to keep his voice low as he got to his feet and crept back to the house so that they were now at the same height. "Can you fit through the window?"

"Can I fit through the window?" she repeated, her eyes narrowing and her lips pursing. "Are you seriously asking me that?"

"It is a reasonable question," he said. "If you can, then come out. We must hurry."

"Clearly," she said. "Hold it open for me?"

He nodded and did so as she put both hands on the window sill and boosted herself up, shimmying forward until half of her body was outside. Keeping one hand holding the window up, he wrapped the other around her waist as he helped her through, trying not to think about how her soft, generous breasts were pressing against his arm.

He didn't realize he was holding his breath until she squirmed in his arms.

"You can put me down now."

"Of course," he said, practically dropping her as he did so. "Let's go."

"Go?" she said with wide eyes. "And just leave them here

so they can return to Castleton, much less happy when they realize I'm gone?"

"What do you suppose us to do?" he asked. "It is us against the four of them."

"Wait until they sleep and then shoot them?"

He stared at her, trying to assess whether or not she was jesting. It was difficult to tell with her.

"I will not shoot unarmed men."

"Even if they kidnapped me?"

"Even so," he said, before pausing. "Did they… harm you?"

"No," she said, her voice low and harsh. "I was concerned about the night, however. That is why I escaped."

"Why I saved you."

"You were helpful," she acknowledged, "however I did not need you. I would have escaped regardless."

He snorted, interested in asking her more, but that would have to come later. At the moment, they had greater concerns. He heard another whinny and looked over as it sparked an idea.

"What if we took their horses?" he said.

"Then they couldn't follow us," she said, immediately understanding, her lips curling into a small smile.

"It's a bit of a risk as their horses are closer to the house."

"But worth it," she said.

Gideon went over and untied his own horse so that he would be ready and waiting, and then began approaching the others.

"Wait here," he told Madeline quietly, but of course, she didn't listen and followed, helping him untie them, and he watched her out of the corner of his eye as she crooned softly to the horses while she did so. Who was he to question her methods, however, when the horse nuzzled his nose into Madeline's neck?

Gideon took the reins of three of the horses, Madeline

THE HEIR'S FORTUNE

the other two, and they began to lead them away from the house, praying that they would stay relatively silent.

They had neared the break in the trees that separated the cottage from the road beyond when there was a creak behind them and the front door swung open.

"Ay! ¿Quién está ahí?"

Gideon looked over at Madeline, surprised when, instead of appearing worried, she grinned at him.

"Well, they want to know who is here," she said, shocking him as she nearly fluidly swung herself onto a horse. *"¡Vámanos!"*

* * *

GIDEON'S HORSE thundered alongside Madeline's, their bodies in sync as they raced through the trees. Exhilaration surged through Madeline, her hair whipping wildly behind her as they stayed just ahead of their pursuers. She couldn't help but admire Gideon's skill as he deftly guided his horse, the two of them seamlessly navigating the twists and turns of the forest.

The thrill of the chase pulsed through her veins, a stark contrast to the suffocating fear of being trapped in the cabin. But now, with Gideon by her side and the rush of freedom propelling them forward, she felt truly alive.

Suddenly, a gunshot shattered the peaceful sounds of hooves on dirt. But Gideon was unshaken, staying close to her as they urged their horses even faster. The other four horses followed suit, running as if driven by their own desire for escape.

Through it all, Gideon remained focused, expertly leading them down a path unknown to Madeline. As they rode on for over an hour, she couldn't help but feel grateful for his presence and his unwavering determination to keep them safe.

"We should stop," he said, his breath slightly faster than usual.

"Stop?" she repeated. "Here?"

"This is as good of a place as any. I have a sense of where we are, but we are still at least an hour away from Castleton. There is a stream nearby – do you hear it?" He paused for her to listen and she nodded when she heard the trickle. "We will have to cross it but I would not want the horses to do so in the dark. If their footing slips, we could lose them."

It warmed her heart that he was concerned about horses that should have no bearing on him. Unlike many of the men she knew, he saw them as more than just property.

"What do you suggest?"

"Your captors will not be able to catch us tonight if they are on foot, nor would they be able to track us, even if they are skilled, in the dark. Daylight will greet us in but a few hours. We should camp here, catch a few hours of sleep, and then continue on in the early morning."

She nodded, trying to still her body as a shiver caught her, not wanting him to see any sign of weakness that she might not be able to do as he wished.

But, of course, being Gideon, he noticed.

"You're cold," he said.

"A bit," she admitted. "But I will be fine."

"I have a blanket and a flask of water in my saddlebag, but that is all for provisions as I left in such haste, I'm afraid," he said. "I shall try to make a fire, but it will be difficult in the dark."

"No need."

He shook his head. "There is. Always share the truth with me, Madeline."

His voice seemed to have lowered an octave, and it caused

a strange sensation in Madeline's stomach. Why was he suddenly appealing to her so?

She had never thought him to be a knight in shining armor, nor had she needed his rescue, and yet… the fact that he had come for her had caused her to see him in a different light.

"Very well. I am slightly cold, but I shall be fine. I still have my cloak."

She shifted it around her shoulders, realizing as she did so that her skirt was still hiked up around her waist from riding astride, although Gideon likely hadn't been able to see anything in the dark.

"Where did you learn to ride like that?" he asked as though to prove her wrong.

"My father," she said. "It was just the two of us in our family, and he was a proficient rider and often took me with him on his journeys. I do usually ride side saddle, but he taught me to ride astride when I was a girl."

"I've heard stories of your father," Gideon commented, and Madeline listened for judgment in his tone but heard none.

"I'm not surprised," she intoned. She wasn't one who usually shared much with others, but she didn't see any harm in telling Gideon more of her early life. He was not such a gossip.

"His life turned out nothing as he planned," she continued. "He was a second son who thought he could live as he pleased, and then he inherited a title he didn't want and lost the wife he loved. He did his best with what he had left."

"He did well," Gideon said, and Madeline started.

"Is that a compliment?"

"It's the truth. I told you – I always speak the truth."

A strange warmth ran through her at his words, despite the cold.

As Gideon laid the blanket on the ground and set up camp, Madeline walked around the horses, praising them for their escape and fine running. If she had to guess from their sleek hair, healthy weight, and extravagant saddles, the four of them were a set. They wore English saddles, which meant that they had been taken here on English soil. She doubted they had been purchased and they were too fine of horseflesh to have been hired out.

It made her hate the men more than for capturing her.

A slight crack caught her attention, and she turned to find Gideon sitting back on his haunches, intent on the ground before him.

"You did it!" Madeline said, her jaw dropping open as she came to crouch beside him, watching as the small flame flickered in front of them.

"It's not much," he said wryly, "but it is something."

"It's damp here," she said, feeling the ground around them. "It might be hard to find enough dry wood for a larger fire."

He stood and walked over to a nearby tree, breaking off a few smaller branches.

"This is green so it won't work well, but it's dry enough that hopefully it will help," he said, placing them around the small fire, which grew just enough to light up his face. Madeline wasn't sure that she had ever noted just how angular his features were, how dark and sensual his eyes could be. He wore so many expressions on that face, but few were ever anything but tense and rigid.

Madeline held her hands out over the fire to encourage warmth back into her fingers, and suddenly his eyes narrowed, one of his hands shooting out and grasping her arm that was no longer covered by her cloak.

"You told me that they didn't hurt you."

He was staring at the angry red welts on her arms, and she was caught off guard by the intensity of his gaze.

"I partially did it to myself," she said, her voice low as she recounted her experience, which she was aware could have been far worse than it had been. "They tied me to the bed, at first quite tightly. They released me to write the note to you, still believing I was Cassandra. The man who retied me was much more sympathetic than the rest of them. When he returned me to the room, I told him the binds were too tight the first time and he agreed to tie them with more slack. I couldn't quite free my hands right away but had to work them against the wood of the bed until I could loosen them enough to slip them through."

His eyes were hard, icier than she had ever seen them.

"Perhaps you were right," he said, surprising her with the growl in his tone.

"Right in what?" she asked, her breath catching, although why, she had no idea.

"I should have killed them."

CHAPTER 9

*G*ideon knew he was being an ass as he prowled around their makeshift campsite, searching for more wood to build the fire to keep her warm.

It was not as though she was irrevocably harmed. A few welts were nothing that a proper ointment wouldn't fix. And yet, the thought that the men had had their hands on her, that she had been vulnerable to them, had him seething with restless energy, even though he knew, rationally, that she was here and safe with him now.

He had to be sure to keep her that way.

"Gideon?"

He was immediately drawn to the soft, husky timbre of her voice. It stirred emotions within him that he had never before encountered.

Which was exactly why he always strove to avoid her.

"We should sleep," she said, speaking softly, completely unaware of the effect she was having on him. "Tomorrow we shall have lots of explaining to do, and we will have to go to the proper authorities to have them find these men."

"Do you think it was *Don* Rafael?"

Faith and Lord Ferrington had been chased by the Spaniard earlier in the year after they had stolen the map from his estate in San Sebastian. The fact that it had been within his family's possession gave him cause to believe the treasure was meant to be his. According to the man's servant, however, the treasure was never the Palencia family's to begin with.

"He must have sent them," Gideon said. "We will have to determine where he is right now. Whether he is still jailed or if he has escaped."

Gideon could barely see her in the dim light that surrounded them from the paltry fire he had created and the glimpses of moonlight from above, but he could sense the hunch in her shoulders.

"Take the blanket," he said, gesturing toward it, and she sank gratefully upon it, although she didn't lie down.

"What will you do?"

"I'll keep watch."

"You said you didn't think that we would be in any danger."

"I don't," he said, for the truth was he wanted to allow her to sleep alone. They shouldn't be here just the two of them as it was, but he was sure that this would be forgiven due to the circumstances. If he was to sleep next to her, it might be different.

At least, that's what he told himself.

Although there was a greater reason that he didn't want to explore – the fact that he might *want* there to be more, and those emotions would be impossible to ignore if they were in such an intimate setting as lying next to one another.

"Very well," she said as she lay down, wrapping the blanket around her.

Gideon tugged his cloak closer as he sat, leaning against a thick tree trunk, the fallen leaves creating a soft carpet beneath him. At least Madeline should likely be comfortable, as an earthy scent filled the air around them.

There was a damp crispness to the air, and Gideon wasn't sure if it was because they had stopped moving or if it was simply the time of night, but the temperature had dropped. He shivered as he allowed his eyes to close for a moment, the high alertness that had filled him for the entirety of the day dropping but an inch.

The leaves rustled in the trees around him as the cold breeze still found him, even in the dense thicket they found themselves in.

An owl's call echoed through the sky, an answering howl resounding, to which one of the horse's nervously whinnied in response and pawed the ground.

"It's all right," Gideon called out softly, hoping to soothe the animal. "They're far from us."

Whether he was reassuring the animals or Madeline, he wasn't certain, but when he glanced her way, he could tell from the tense hold of her body that she was not yet sleeping.

He squinted in the dark. She was only a few feet from him, and as he moved closer to her, he realized that she wasn't just tense – she was shaking.

"Madeline?" he said in a low voice. "Are you all right?"

"Fine," she said, but the word was garbled, and around it, he heard the chattering of her teeth against one another.

"You are not fine," he said, tentatively reaching out a hand and placing it on her back, surprised by how much she was moving beneath it. "Are you cold?"

"Yes," she said, inhaling a breath swiftly. "Cold."

Gideon paused for a moment, uncertain of just what he should do. He knew what seemed to be the *right* course of action, and he was more than aware of what his body wanted to do – he just wasn't sure if he should.

But there was one person he knew who never seemed to hesitate, who was as self-assured as anyone he had ever met.

"Madeline?"

"Yes?"

"Would you like me to lie with you? F-for warmth?"

He sounded like a nervous schoolboy. Hopefully she would think he was just cold himself.

"Would you mind?" she said as she lay the blanket back out beside her.

Would he mind? Not at all.

He slowly eased himself onto the blanket, shimmying so that her back was to his front. He had barely made any contact with her when she sank back against him, burying herself into him. He was a tall man, standing a good head above her, and she fit perfectly within the circle of his body as he tucked his knees beneath hers and lay first his cloak and then his blanket over top of her.

He wasn't entirely sure what to do with his arm, but then she grabbed it and wrapped it tightly around her waist with no seeming intent to release it, so he succumbed and relaxed it against her.

"Better?" he asked, and she nodded against him, still shivering but perhaps not quite so forcefully.

"B-better," she said.

She was soft in his arms, and Gideon wondered whether she had ever made herself so vulnerable to another before. He liked to think that he was special, in this if nothing else.

Her soft hair tickled his chin, and he tipped his head so that he could bury his nose in the spicy scent of the strands, which had lost any pins that had been in place earlier in the day.

"Gideon?"

"Yes?" he replied, grateful that her teeth were no longer chattering as they had been.

"I am sorry that you didn't find your treasure today."

With all that had happened, he had nearly forgotten that today was the day he had thought he would find the treasure, putting an end to this hunt that had captivated them all for over a year now.

He found, however, that he was not nearly as chagrined as he thought he'd be.

"You are safe," he said. "That is what matters most."

"I was only ever in danger due to my own stubborn stupidity," she said bitterly.

"You would have been safer had you stayed in the house, yes," he agreed. "But I am sure they would have found some way to capture you – or Cassandra."

"If I must be grateful for anything, it is that they didn't take Cassandra," she said softly. "She has the baby – and she has been through enough already."

Gideon stiffened at her words.

"What do you know about what Cassandra has been through?" he forced himself to ask.

Madeline snorted. "Being sent away to an institution to change her scandalous ways when she had done nothing but find love and begin to explore her passions?"

Gideon was lost for words as a crushing weight seemed to fall upon him. So Cassandra had told Madeline. He had wondered but had always hoped no one else knew of his greatest mistake.

"I never should have sent her away," he said in a low voice, the shame of that decision still haunting him. "That night... after Mother found Cassandra in her state of undress, she was determined that something must be done. She didn't want my father to know and I was the last person to have any idea of how to deal with a willful young woman. Cassandra is only two years younger than I."

"So..."

He let out a heavy sigh. "So we went to those who had advised us all my life."

"The men who lost all of your family's wealth."

He let out a humorless laugh. "Those would be the ones. Of course, we didn't know it at the time."

"Yet still, you allowed others to settle Cassandra's fate. She is your *sister*."

"I know," he said quietly. "And I would do anything to take it back but I cannot change the past. Instead, I have done all I can to improve her future."

"Then why did you make it so difficult for her to marry your best friend?"

"I had no issue with her marrying Devon until I found out he was the one who had ruined her," Gideon said, leaning his head back to look up at the few stars that twinkled through the trees. "It was all a mad miscommunication. But, thankfully, they have both forgiven me and one another and we have moved on from it."

She made a strangled sound, and his arm tightened ever so slightly.

"What does that mean?"

"Nothing."

He realized what it was, and it made his heart sink even lower. "You hate me for it."

"I do not *hate* you—"

"I understand. I hate myself for it too. At least you didn't lie to me. Now get some sleep."

"Gideon—"

"Sleep. There is not much time until the light returns and then we will be hastening home."

"Very well," she said, and it didn't take long for her to begin relaxing in his arms, sinking more heavily into him. Gideon was not sure that he would ever be able to sleep, but he would take these moments of rest and appreciate the beauty of the woman in his arms.

Madeline was never without her opinions, that was for certain. Even if she had nothing to say, there was always the quirk of her lips, a raised eyebrow, or an amused grin at the ready. He had never seen her so defenseless, as trusting as she was in his arms right now.

And he was enjoying it far more than he should be, even with the knowledge of her opinion of him.

He knew that he should be staying alert, to ensure their safety if nothing else.

Then his eyes were closing, and he thought it should be fine if he rested them – just for one moment.

The next thing he knew, he was surrounded by light, although it was a dim light through the misty fog that shrouded them, casting an ethereal glow on the world where they had slept.

They. He looked down at where Madeline was supposed to be lying next to him.

She was gone.

CHAPTER 10

Madeline hummed a sombre tune as she finished splashing cold water from the stream onto her face, the melody matching the atmosphere of the day as an ethereal mist was rising over the water in front of her.

This place was magical.

But then, Castleton always had been, and they had to be nearby.

She was so intent on the peacefulness of her surroundings that she jumped and whirled around at the crack of a fallen tree branch, sighing in relief when she saw that Gideon was standing near, his eyes intent upon her.

"Good morning," she called.

"Good morning," he said as he walked toward her now, his legs easily eating up the ground in front of him.

"I was wondering where you were," Gideon said, running a hand over his face, and it was only then she realized what he must be thinking.

"Where did you think I could have gone?" she asked, tilting her head and placing her fists on her hips. "I do not know the land, nor have I a compass or any provisions. Like it or not, I am stuck with you."

"Am I really so bad?"

His words were soft, almost inaudible amidst the chirping of birds around them and Madeline found herself strangely drawn closer to him despite all the reasons the two of them made no sense together. He caught her eyes, and that deep glow she had noticed before seemed to present itself again, everything else vanishing but the two of them in this small forest thicket as her heart beat so loudly against the wall of her chest she was certain he must be able to hear it.

She didn't want to break the spell, but as much as his gaze held her frozen in place – an invisible tether connecting them – she knew she had to put a stop to it before either of them assumed any ideas that should never be.

"I didn't say you were bad," she attempted, lifting her cloak to dry her face when she realized that water was running down the side of it.

"No, you didn't," he agreed. "But I am sure, if you had the choice, I would not be the man you would be out here with."

She considered his words as she lifted her boot – thank goodness she and Cassandra had dressed for walking yesterday morning – and stubbed it into the dirt.

"Perhaps a few days ago, I would have said that," she admitted. "But you have surprised me."

"Surprising is not often a word used to describe me."

"Well, after riding to my rescue and then sleeping next to me all night, I would say you deserve it."

"About that," he said, clearing his throat. "If you feel that I have ruined your reputation in any way—"

"Of course not," she said with a snort. "I was the one who asked you to provide me warmth. That was all. Not only are these circumstances far from ordinary, but no one else knows of what happened besides you and me."

"But if you feel I compromised you—"

"Gideon," she said stepping closer to him, lifting a hand to cup his cheek, "if I were to be compromised, then a lot more would have happened than sleeping next to one another."

She watched his pupils dilate, knowing her meaning was clear as he swallowed hard.

"I would never—"

"Yes, that part is certainly not surprising," she said wryly before tilting her head as she studied him. "Did it even occur to you?"

"Did what, exactly, occur to me?"

"To compromise me."

She had no idea what had spurred her on to ask him such a thing, but last night, as she had lain in his arms, she hadn't been able to help but enjoy how it felt to be wrapped in his embrace. She never thought she would have actually fallen asleep outdoors, especially after all she had been through that day, but there was a strange sense of comfort with Gideon and she had drifted off quite quickly.

She had awoken when the sun began to peek through the trees and had been distinctly aware of Gideon behind her. For the first time, she saw him not at all as Cassandra's brother but rather… a man. An attractive, virile, protective man who had been there for her in a way that no one ever had been before.

Her father had been the only true adult presence in her life, but she could never be completely certain as to whether or not he would be called away for the next party or game or event, and she would be left behind with a string of governesses, none of whom could keep up with her and her antics.

She hadn't been the best of children.

In fact, the gentlemen now stayed away from her for the

very same reasons governesses had. She was too dramatic. Too forthright. Too... *much*.

Everyone shied away from her.

But Gideon hadn't.

He had stayed and he had been there for her, even when he likely wasn't certain if he was being true to himself and his morals. She might not have needed saving, but it had been nice to have someone try.

He didn't flinch when she spoke her mind, but instead seemed to take it all in stride. His steady presence came as something of a relief, even as he was surprisingly more enigmatic than she had ever given him credit for.

His blue eyes blazed as he stared down at her, and she reached out, lacing her fingers through his as she stepped closer to him.

"I wouldn't have minded if you had compromised me last night," she said quietly, the words coming out just as she realized them herself. His eyes widened in shock as he jerked in surprise, but he did not seem at all repulsed. Instead he seemed... interested. Before she could think better of it, Madeline stood on the tips of her toes and pressed a gentle kiss against his lips before pulling away.

"Thank you," she whispered, moving but an inch away from his face. "For everything."

Gideon stared at her, his eyes moving from one of her eyes to the next, before he gripped the back of her head with one of his large hands and then pulled her in close, kissing her once more.

Madeline's heart swelled in her chest as his lips moved over hers, the kiss deepening and Gideon's grip on her head tightening. His free hand moved to rest on her waist, his fingertips tracing circles against the fabric of her dress through her cloak. How could a touch through so many layers still feel so intimate? She moaned into his mouth, pressing herself closer to him as the fire between them ignited further.

He pulled away abruptly, confusion in his eyes before he stepped away from her completely. Madeline blinked up at him, caught off guard by the intensity of their kiss – and his reaction, which was as though he regretted it the instance it had occurred.

"I—" he began, and she prepared herself to stop him before he could apologize. She was, after all, the one who started this. Instead, he just shook his head with a small smile before he walked away without another word.

Madeline watched him go, warmth spreading through her limbs. She looked around her, taking in the beauty of her surroundings and the moment they had just shared, before she touched a hand to her lips as she slowly followed him back to the campsite, wondering what would happen next between them – and if he would ever allow it again.

* * *

GIDEON CHOSE to say nothing about their kiss as they packed up their campsite and gathered the horses. She had taken him by surprise, that was for certain – but it was his own reaction that most shocked him. Once he had a taste of her, he had become a man possessed and hadn't been able to stop himself from going back for more.

Now he wondered how he would ever forget how magical she was, how soft her lips were, how lush her mouth was.

Then there was how perfect she had felt lying in the crook of his body all night. She was a mystery, this woman, and one that he was enjoying solving – which surprised him more than anyone or anything else ever could. He had thought that he was always on edge around her because he wasn't sure what to expect.

Maybe the tension was for another reason altogether.

He had to be certain, however, not to allow himself to become too attached. As much as he had placed great hopes upon turning up a treasure that would solve everything for him and his family, there was a good possibility that this would come to nothing, and he would be left with no choice but to marry for a dowry.

Which was one thing he knew that Madeline most decidedly did not have.

"Did you hear them speak of *Don* Rafael?" he asked Madeline now as they mounted their horses and turned them toward Castleton, the four remaining horses following them.

"I heard his name a few times, but unfortunately my Spanish is not good enough for me to have understood anything else," she said.

"I do wonder how he orchestrated this when he was in English custody," Gideon murmured.

"He must have been released," Madeline said. "It would be difficult to hold a Spanish nobleman, would it not?"

"It would," he agreed. "I just thought that I would have been notified if that had happened."

"Well, once we return to Castleton, hopefully, we can make sense of it all," she said. "How was Cassandra?"

"Distraught that you had been taken. I didn't tell her that the men thought that you were her for it would likely only make things worse."

"Good idea," she said with a smile, one that made him feel like he was the most profound man on earth, especially as he knew that her smiles were not readily given out. "I didn't tell them the truth for I didn't want them returning to take Cassandra instead." She tilted her head. "Would you have given up the map for me?"

"If it had come to that, yes," Gideon said truthfully. No treasure was worth anyone's life. "But I didn't want them returning to my land for any reason so I am glad it didn't come to that."

She nodded, a thoughtful expression on her face.

"What will you do once we return to Castleton?" he asked, feigning nonchalance, but the truth was, he was much more interested in her response than he would ever want her to know.

"I am not sure," she said, crinkling her nose. "I suppose it depends how much longer Cassandra has need of me."

"You are not concerned?"

"Concerned about what?"

"The danger," he said. "After all that happened, I wouldn't blame you if you decided to get as far away from Castleton – and from us – as you could."

She lifted a brow. "Is that what you want?"

It wasn't. Not at all. In fact, he was enjoying this time together far more than he should. He could see himself spending more time with her, which was something he had never considered with a woman.

"I do not want you to be in danger again," he said, telling the truth.

She laughed lightly. "Well, I am at Castleton until my father comes to collect me, for it is apparently too dangerous for me to travel on my own – which is ironic, is it not?"

"I will keep you safe now," he said fiercely. "I promise."

She met his eyes.

"I believe you."

He would make sure of it. Protecting his family had always been more important than anything, including finding this treasure or rebuilding the family's fortune. But in this short time with Madeline, she had become important to him as well. Which scared him more than he would like to admit.

He wondered, once they returned to Castleton, just how much he would continue to see her – and when he did, would everything go back to the way it had been, with the two of them passing acquaintances tied to one another only through Cassandra, or would she recognize as much as he had that everything had changed between them?

Gideon wasn't much for change – not unless it was change that he had planned for and orchestrated, such as the gift of the treasure hunt that had appeared like an answer to all his prayers.

Madeline was a gift that he wasn't prepared for but seemed inclined to overtake him anyway. If he were to go down this path, however, he would have no choice but to find this treasure.

His friends would tell him that she was worth the risk. His sister surely would as well.

He was the last man to ever leave anything to chance.

But maybe he had finally found something – or someone – to risk it all for.

CHAPTER 11

"Madeline!"

Cassandra came racing down the steps of Castleton toward them the moment they neared the front entrance, in a most unladylike display of excitement that reminded Madeline of all of the reasons she so dearly loved her friend.

She was only just beaten in her race to them by Scout, who came bounding down the stairs after her, running to Gideon and Madeline and alternating between jumping upon them and licking their faces. If Madeline didn't know better, she would have said he had grown already in the two days she had been away.

She scratched his head, telling him what a good boy he was before Cassandra drew her attention away with her questions.

"You're alive. Thank goodness. Are you hurt? What happened? Did Gideon find you? Why did it take so long for you to return home?"

Madeline couldn't help but laugh at the barrage of questions, and she took Cassandra's hands within hers to calm her.

"I am not hurt. It is a long story that we will tell you when we are all together. Gideon did find me, yes, as I was escaping the captors. And we stopped overnight because we didn't want to lead all of the horses across the stream in the dark."

Cassandra nodded before peering beyond Madeline, finding her brother.

"Thank you, Gideon," she said simply, and he nodded at her.

"Of course," he said, before leading all of the horses toward the stables without another word to her, Scout trotting happily after him, the only one of the pair to turn around to look at Madeline.

Was that it, then? Was all that had happened between them to come to nothing now that they had returned? Madeline knew he wasn't a man much given over to emotion, nor to chance, but she was surely going to be having a word with him over what was to be expected now.

Cassandra was unable to wait to hear the entirety of the story, so Madeline told her bits of it as they entered Castleton and Cassandra sat with her while the maids prepared a warm bath, which Madeline gratefully sank into. As the water warmed her, she couldn't help but think of the last time she had been warmed, but by Gideon's arms, his body against her, her bottom against his—

"Were you surprised when Gideon came after you?" Cassandra asked, causing Madeline to jerk with a start. What was wrong with her? She was lusting after her best friend's brother while Cassandra sat next to her, oblivious to what had happened in that part of the rescue. Madeline had no intentions of ever telling her – not unless anything more were to come of it.

Did she want there to be more?

Perhaps.

She had always held such a grudge against Gideon, but she had been able to see things partially from his side when he had explained what had happened with Cassandra. Not only that, but he had seemed contrite and appeared to be doing what he could to make it right.

Madeline had also always assumed that he was trying to control everyone around him – but perhaps he was just trying to keep them safe.

"Yes, I was surprised," she said, answering Cassandra's question. "He never quite seemed the savior type to me."

"I can see why you might think that," Cassandra said. "But that is exactly who he is, just in his own way. He is trying to save our family with this treasure hunt. When he sent me away, he was only doing what he thought was best at the time, even if he was wrong. And he would hear no other option but to go after you himself, for he had to ensure that you were safe."

Madeline swallowed as her opinion of him grew evermore. This was not what she needed to hear. Not if she was trying to keep herself away from him.

There was no question about it. She was going to have to determine if he felt anything for her, or if he had been caught up in the moment.

The idea that there could be something between them caused a spark of excitement to ignite within her chest – a spark that she hadn't felt in some time, and certainly hadn't expected when it came to Gideon Sutcliffe.

"Why are you smiling like that?"

"Pardon me?" Madeline asked, her gaze whipping over to her friend.

"You look as though you are particularly… pleased about something. Or perhaps excited."

"I'm just happy to be back," Madeline said. "Actually, I am rather tired. If you don't mind—"

"Of course!" Cassandra said, standing immediately. "I am so sorry. I only wanted to make sure you were well. When I asked you to Castleton, I never considered that there would be any danger, though I should have after all that has previously occurred. If I hadn't—"

"Cassandra," Madeline said firmly. "You are as bad as your brother. This is no one's fault but the men who took me. Now, all will be well. I just need to bathe and sleep and then I will come down and eat a hearty dinner and all will be right in the world."

"Very well," Cassandra said. "If you need anything—"

"I will let you know. Of course."

Madeline closed her eyes and shook her head fondly as Cassandra retreated out the door. She knew that her friend would forever blame herself for what happened. If only she could understand that Madeline would do anything to keep her safe – her and her family.

There seemed to be a lot of protecting going on around here.

But she supposed that was what happened when you cared for someone.

Madeline tried to deny that she was dressing with extra care that evening. She had all the same clothing that she had before. But now when she donned her favorite navy gown, she added an extra bit of jewellery with a locket that had been her mother's and she was more particular with her hair. Her poor maid had to refasten some of her pins three times over until Madeline was pleased with the results.

Perhaps it was because of Gideon, although why he would see her any differently than he had before now, she had no idea. He didn't seem particularly affected by their time together, and she had been the forward one – she had likely been far too much for him, as was usually the case with most men she met.

Cassandra's husband, Lord Covington, greeted her with an enthusiastic welcome before the four of them sat down to dinner, the duke and duchess declining to join them that evening.

"As much as I enjoy Mother and Father's company, I am glad that we are alone tonight so that we can discuss what happened," Gideon said. He was looking particularly fine tonight himself, with his dark jacket and waistcoat that Madeline mightily approved of. He would cut a dashing figure as the hero in one of her gothic novels – not the happy ones her friends enjoyed, but the dark, broody ones she preferred. "The men who took Madeline were Spanish, and she heard them mention *Don* Rafael. I have sent a letter to determine whether or not he is still in custody. While we may have taken the men's horses, they are still free and could be a threat once more. We must be ready."

Cassandra and Devon exchanged a look.

"Well," Cassandra said slowly, "it is a good thing that help is on the way."

"What does that mean?" Gideon asked, instantly wary.

"When Madeline went missing, I might have written to our friends to tell them what happened and to ask for their help," Cassandra said, cringing slightly.

"Cassandra," Gideon said, rubbing his forehead. "Why would you do that? We are already trying to keep you and Madeline safe, and now there will be more women—"

"Who are all very self-sufficient," Madeline cut in, unable to help herself. "Besides, the extra gentlemen will be of help, will they not?"

Gideon sighed, his long fingers stroking his glass of port.

"I suppose you are right."

"Gideon, you do not have to do all of this yourself,"

Cassandra said. "We are all here for you, and our friends are coming because they want to help us."

Gideon sighed. "I suppose we best wait for everyone to arrive, then, before we go searching for the treasure, should we not?"

"It makes the most sense," Cassandra said, even as her eyes lit up at the thought of all of them doing this together. "Besides, we would not want to find the treasure only for Madeline's captors to re-appear and steal it from us. It has been hidden for this long now – why not allow it to remain where it is until the timing is perfect?"

"You have a point," Gideon said, rubbing his forehead, and Madeline had a strange urge to lean forward and kiss away the wrinkle that marred it.

The footman came in and cleared away their near-untouched first course, replacing it with the second, which was a mystery meat covered in a soupy white sauce. At least the peas and potatoes beside it appeared appetizing enough.

"I'm sorry," Gideon said, whispering low, before looking from one side to the other to make sure he wasn't overheard. "I know the food is terrible, but the cook's family has been with us for generations. She's still learning, and I keep hoping that she'll improve but..." he tossed his hands up in the air. Madeline speared the peas and tried them, finding that they were mediocre but certainly edible.

"She has done well with the peas," she said, to which Cassandra snorted, causing a most unladylike display as she had a mouth full of claret that she had to fight to contain. Madeline started to laugh as well, and soon enough both of them were bent over, tears escaping their eyes.

Gideon and Devon watched them for a minute with incredulous expressions, before Devon was the first to give in with a chuckle, Gideon following soon afterward, until all four of them were laughing so hard that they didn't notice the footman enter.

When one came to remove the meals, Gideon waved him away.

"We're still working on this," he said, to which the footman nodded, and finally their laughter subsided enough that they continued eating what they could of the meal.

Madeline sat back in her chair, looking around at the three of them. She was enjoying this. She had never had much of a family. Her father was family, yes, but he had never been around very often, and when he had been, he did not have a great deal of interest in spending time with a child. As she grew, he treated her more as an inconvenience he had to be rid of.

She had hoped that when she married, she would find someone who she could get along with if nothing else. She wasn't sure what kind of mother she would be, but she did long to have people in her life who cared for her and whom she cared for in turn.

Was this what it would be like, such as the time she was spending with these people here?

It scared her how much she was enjoying this, as there was a large part of her that knew she might only be showing herself just how much she would miss once it was all gone.

CHAPTER 12

Castleton was his inheritance as well as his responsibility, and yet Gideon still found himself creeping down the staircase as though he was sneaking out without wanting his parents or schoolmaster to be aware.

It was not that he was breaking any rules.

It was that he was starving, and he didn't want to wake anyone – nor offend them.

The kitchen was, thankfully, empty at this time of night, his only company being Scout, who had followed him carefully down the stairs, toenails clicking, and was currently lying at his feet awaiting any food scraps that might come his way.

Gideon entered the larder, searching within until he found what he was looking for.

Chicken – he thought. Some kind of meat, anyway, that appeared to be cooked but not yet covered in any sauce.

He sank his teeth into it, unable to stop his groan of pleasure. A whine at his feet reminded him of his friend, and he broke off a piece of the meat and tossed it to the dog, who caught it in delight.

"Delicious, isn't it?" Gideon said, returning to look for anything else that might be edible. He found some cranberry sauce, backing out with it in hand, but when he walked right into something soft behind him, he was so startled that he tossed it in the air.

Hands reached out and grabbed the bowl before it could fall, and he turned around in shock, still tightly clutching the chicken leg.

"Madeline?" he mumbled around the meat, and she smirked as she turned and placed the bowl of cranberry sauce on the table, the hem of her wrapper giving him peeks of her bare feet below.

"Hungry?" she asked, and he nodded woodenly as she reached down to pet Scout before searching through drawers until she found a spoon and started to help herself. "I know you have loyalty, and that is an admirable quality, but you are all going to starve yourselves at this rate."

"I know," he said with a sigh.

"You do not have to be rid of the woman," she said with a shrug. "Perhaps just find a position for which she would be more suited."

"True," he said, considering her words, uncertain why he hadn't figured that out for himself. "I would still have to find – and pay – a cook."

"Your mother would help with that, would she not?" Madeline asked, turning around and leaning back against the wooden counter as she looked at him. "That is a role for the lady of the house."

"My mother has much on her mind," he said. "I try not to bother her with such things."

"You need a wife then," Madeline said, her eyes gleaming, and Gideon couldn't help but watch the way the silver spoon ran over her lips.

"Y-yes," he stammered, losing the ability to think properly. Was that her goal here? "I have been aware of that for some time. I was waiting to discover what treasure awaited."

"What does the treasure have to do with finding a wife?" she asked with a frown, and Gideon paused, uncertain of how much to tell her. To say it aloud sounded so superficial, and yet it was not as though it was his choice – it was simply how things were.

He leaned back against the wall behind him, throwing Scout the rest of the chicken without the bone. He was aware that he was only wearing his nightshirt and wrapper as well. It seemed too familiar to be in such a state of undress together, and yet it was also strangely natural as well.

"You know about the state of the dukedom," he said as fact instead of a question, for he knew that Cassandra shared most everything with her.

"I do."

"And you know I have been hoping that this treasure will help us restore our fortunes to what they need to be in order to look after our properties and our people?"

"Of course." A light dawned in her eyes as she met his. "You will marry to restore that fortune instead."

"If I must."

"Cassandra never mentioned that was your plan, but it makes perfect sense. It is what most do," she murmured. Gideon didn't miss the look in her eyes, only he wasn't sure if he was misreading it or only hoping for something more.

"Why have you not done so already?"

He had to look away then, for the truth was not one he had an interest in readily sharing.

"To be honest, I had always hoped I would have the opportunity to find someone who could be like a... partner to me."

"A partner," she repeated. "Knowing you, by a partner, you mean someone who could help you look after everything, who is practical and knowledgeable and understands the workings of the dukedom?"

That was not it at all. The truth was, he was hoping he might find someone he could love, who would love him in turn, but the notion was so fanciful that he couldn't say it aloud. He barely admitted it to himself.

"Something like that," was what he murmured instead.

"I see," she said. "As it happens, I need to marry as well, but unfortunately I do not have the fortune you are looking for."

He smiled ruefully. "I know."

"Oh, you have considered me, then?"

His eyes shot up, meeting hers, uncertain of what the meaning was behind her words.

"What is happening here, Madeline?" he asked in a low voice.

"Do you mean between us?"

"Yes."

"I was going to ask you the same thing," she said, looking up at him from beneath her thick, dark eyelashes. "One moment you are kissing me in the woods, the next you are walking away from me as though nothing happened."

"I wasn't sure if it was something you would want to revisit or forget about."

"I would never have kissed you first if I didn't want anything more to occur," she said, with a smile as she took a couple of steps toward him. "I just need to know if you kissed me back out of obligation or desire."

His breath came faster the closer she moved. Her long dark hair was currently loose and free around her shoulders and he lifted his hand to run his fingers through it, waiting for her to pull back and away from him, but instead, she only leaned in,

"I do many things out of obligation, Madeline," he said, his voice hoarse. "Kissing you is not one of them."

He leaned down, then, cupping her head with his hands as he lowered his lips to hers. She was soft, lush, and pillowy, and he drank her in, his senses alive with the taste of her and the cranberries she had just finished. The kiss was a slow dance, one that spoke of longing for more. Heat radiated from Madeline's body, her warmth seeping into Gideon's very soul.

The delicate brush of her tongue intertwined with his, igniting a fire within him. Time seemed to stand still as they lost themselves to one another.

Gideon's hands tangled in her ebony locks before tracing a path down her neck, caressing every inch of exposed skin. His fingers danced along the contours of her spine, leaving a trail of tingling sensations that made her shudder beneath his touch.

Madeline's body molded into his, her curves fitting perfectly against his lean frame. The scent of her hair, a heady mix of jasmine and vanilla, invaded his senses, and he wondered how he had missed noticing this woman for so long.

He had thought her trouble, but she was proving to be trouble of the best kind. A distraction from his responsibilities, yes, but had a distraction been exactly what he needed?

She moaned, tilting her head backward to accept more of his kiss, and he circled his hands around her ribcage so that his thumbs were splayed beneath her breasts.

"Gideon," she whispered into his mouth, her breathing ragged, and he boosted her up onto the countertop behind her, knocking the cranberry sauce off the table and to the floor.

"We should stop," he murmured.

"Likely," she agreed, although neither of them made any

move to do so. Instead, he slid his hands upward, cupping her breasts from beneath, and she answered by arching her chest toward him.

He had thought he barely knew her, but the truth was, now that he allowed himself to be *aware* of her, he discovered that he knew her far better than he ever would have guessed.

She was humorous and saw the dark and light of everything she encountered – including him. No one else had ever seen both sides of him before and not only put up with them but appreciated them.

And he wanted her more than he had ever wanted anything in his life – including Castleton.

Which was terrifying. For everything he had ever done was for Castleton, or the Sutcliffe name, or the Sheffield title.

He wanted her, yes, but he wanted her to see him and look at him with that same enraptured expression she did when her face was nose down in one of her gothic novels.

He wanted to protect her and make sure she was never taken away or come to any harm ever again.

He deepened the kiss as she ran her hands over the stubble on his cheeks, pulling her face back and away for just a moment.

"Gideon?" she whispered.

"Yes?"

"We are on the table."

"We are."

"The table where the *food* is prepared."

"It's not very good food," he countered, and she giggled before slapping a hand over her mouth, causing him to chuckle himself. For Madeline didn't giggle. She laughed low, deep, throaty laughs, but never giggled.

Perhaps he affected her after all.

"You laughed!" she exclaimed, her eyes lighting up.

"Why is that so shocking?" he asked, frowning at her, and she reached out and eased the furrow between his brow.

"You're always so serious."

"I have much on my mind," he said with a shrug. "But I do laugh when I find something humorous. And I find you most decidedly humorous."

He leaned in and showed her how much he appreciated her with his kiss, sealing his lips over hers and slipping his tongue into her mouth until she made that desperate moan that had him straining for her even more.

Then she was the one who was sliding the ties of his wrapper apart and pushing the sleeves down over his shoulders, her hand searching between the opening for the bare skin of his chest.

He had to breathe deeply to keep himself from falling over the edge too soon because touches from Madeline were doing more for him than he would ever have thought possible.

Gideon was nestled in between her legs, and he stepped back just enough to begin to slide his hand up her bare leg, finding that he enjoyed how her breath caught when he inched ever higher up her thigh.

"Wait," she said, and he immediately slid his hand back and out from under her nightdress.

"I said wait, not stop!" she said, taking hold of his hand, but he was already lifting her from the table and setting her feet back on the floor.

"You are right. This is not the best place for this," he said, taking deep breaths to try to bring himself back into his body.

"I only wanted to say that I do not want you to feel any obligation toward me," Madeline said. "You just finished telling me that you might need to marry for a significant dowry – one which I certainly do not have – and I understand that. Whatever happens between us, I will not expect any promise."

Gideon was trying to think rationally, but his body was telling him an entirely different story than his head was.

"I would never ruin you," he said.

"Of course you wouldn't," she countered. "I can only ruin myself."

He chuckled wryly again. "You would say that."

"It's the truth. I make my own decisions." She grabbed his wrapper and pulled him closer. "And right now, I want you. Why do we not find somewhere that is more comfortable and finish this?"

"You are bad for me."

"On the contrary," she said. "I believe I am very good for you." She grinned. "Have you ever felt more alive?"

No, he hadn't. Certainly not when he was working on the ledgers in frustration, nor even searching for the treasure. Not even when he was undertaking daring activities with his friends.

For the treasure hunting wasn't fun for him. Not like it was for his friends, for whom it was just a game. For him, it was his life. And now it had taken on even greater meaning. For if he didn't find the treasure, he couldn't have Madeline. And that was beginning to seem like the greatest loss of all.

"Upstairs," he said, making his decision as he tied his wrapper before clicking his tongue at Scout, who had just finished his scraps and sat dutifully by Gideon, although his eyes followed Madeline. "Go first and I will follow after."

She nodded, beginning up the stairs before turning around and pointing a finger at him. "Do not disappoint me, Gideon."

Then with a toss of her dark hair, she ran up the stairs, not quite realizing that her flippant words had more meaning to him than he would ever care to admit.

CHAPTER 13

Madeline was not a woman who often doubted herself.

But as she currently sat in Gideon's well-appointed chamber, completely alone, she was beginning to wonder if she had been too optimistic that the side of him open to risks – and to her – would win out over his rational thought.

The large, opulent dark green walls reminded her of their night together out in the forest, oddly enough, though the four-poster bed with its voluminous velvet draperies was nothing like the thin blanket they had slept on.

She had decided to avoid the bed – for now – and had made herself comfortable in one of the scarred yet comfortable mahogany chairs in front of the fireplace. The only problem was that she couldn't help feeling that the tall, handsome man with rather long dark hair in the portrait above the mantel was staring down at her. He didn't seem judgemental, however. Rather... curious.

Madeline stood, unable to sit still any longer as she began to wander the room. She opened the wardrobe, only to find rows of carefully organized men's clothing awaiting her. She couldn't help but take extra time to sniff the sweet, comforting sandalwood scent of Gideon that wafted out. She stopped in front of the gilded-frame mirror, peering at herself, wondering if Gideon truthfully found her attractive, and if he did, why it had taken him so long to realize it. She had known him forever and he had barely glanced at her in the past. Although, she supposed she had not been his biggest enthusiast either.

She lifted one of the books from the pile on the table beside his bed. A candle was still flickering beside it, and she wondered if he found these rather dull historical texts interesting, or if he had been using them to try to lull himself to sleep before his foray downstairs for food. Perhaps she should try one to help with her own insomnia.

A shadow of doubt flickered through her heart just as wavering as the flame of the candle.

She had been certain that he understood her meaning to meet him upstairs.

Apparently, she had been wrong.

* * *

GIDEON PACED UP and down the bedchamber, worried that he was going to be caught.

"Did I misunderstand, Scout?" he asked the dog, who sat watching him, his head going back and forth, following Gideon's pacing. "I wondered if she truly meant it when she asked me to meet her."

He had never felt more alive, and, at the moment, he had no wish to give up what had been the greatest thing to happen to him since finding that slip of paper with the riddle on it – the one that had started all of this.

He hadn't found the treasure yet, but this search had already opened his eyes to what it might be like to be with a woman of one's own choosing. He understood now what his friends had been waxing on and on poetic about.

He sat back down in the delicate green chair that sat in front of a fireplace which was a good deal smaller than his own. He would have to speak with his few staff about making sure that the fires in their guests' suites were built up higher.

Madeline must freeze in here all night.

Gideon couldn't sit still for long and was soon up, pacing again, this time Scout stepping in time with him back and forth. He would have been worried that he was wearing a hole in the rug beneath his feet, but it was too late for that, for the rug was already far more worn than any rug should be in a duke's home. He wasn't sure this one would even be appropriate for the servants' quarters, let alone a guest's chamber.

But, of course, he was in no position to purchase a new one. Not when he should be using that money for another maid or footman or to do something about the crumbling brick at the front entrance. Or to maintain the grounds. Or replace the sofa in the parlor which had holes currently covered with a blanket.

He sighed. This was why he needed Madeline to arrive – and quickly. For without her, his mind would rattle around to all of the places and all of the things that needed attention.

She was able to draw it all away.

She had seemed enthusiastic and her "do not disappoint me" comment led him to believe that she very much wanted him to follow her. Once he had cleaned up their mess in the kitchen, he had found that it wasn't much of a difficult decision to make as his feet took him up the stairs and directly to her bedchamber.

There was one benefit to having very few staff – there

were not many people to worry about encountering along the way.

Now he was here. Alone.

He might have misread the situation. Although, where else could she possibly be?

A thought hit him. Perhaps he hadn't been wrong in his assumption.

Perhaps he had just been wrong in understanding where she had been expecting him.

* * *

Madeline began the agonizing return walk to her bedchamber. It was in the same wing of the house, but down the next corridor – and it meant that she had to walk by Cassandra and Lord Covington's rooms.

She only hoped her friend wouldn't step out and ask what she was doing out here in the middle of the night, for Madeline still didn't have a ready excuse. She supposed she could say that she had been hungry, but even as close as she and Cassandra were, it didn't seem appropriate to complain about the food here.

Even if she and Gideon had done so together – he had been there along with her, so somehow it hadn't seemed like it had counted.

She was walking so stealthily, keeping her movements so controlled, that she wasn't doing a very good job of watching where she was going – until she ran right into a solid object in the middle of the corridor as a small dog pranced around her feet.

"Oo—" she began, but a large hand covered her mouth and her eyes widened as she recognized the scent and looked up to see Gideon staring down at her.

"You were—" she began whispering, but he shook his head and placed a finger over his lips.

She began pointing in one direction, him in the other, until he pressed his lips together, bent down, and lifted her over his shoulder. She was so surprised she had no words but then he was hurrying down the hall, returning her the way she had come.

"Gideon, what are you doing?" she hissed in his ear.

"We had a miscommunication. I do not like miscommunications," he said, his voice low and growly.

"I wouldn't call it that."

"Then what would you call it?"

"You did not do as I said."

That earned her a surprising swat on the rump and she tried to kick him in return, but he held her ankles tight.

"The last time I checked, women do not order around a future duke."

"This one does."

He sighed. "So you do."

They reached his door and in a remarkable move of dexterity, he managed to open it and fit both of them inside, Scout following behind them. Gideon did not ignore the bed at all, but instead strode right over and tossed her down on top of it, the bed linens enveloping her like clouds.

"Scout," Gideon said, his eyes not moving away from her. "On your bed."

He pointed to what Madeline could only assume was a dog bed in the corner and Scout must have gone willingly.

A thrill raced through her from where their eyes were locked on one another down to the very center of her, which throbbed for him so surprisingly and oh so thrillingly.

"Gideon Sutcliffe, I didn't think you had it in you," she murmured as her lips curled upward.

"I am capable of much more than you would ever give me credit for, my lady," he responded, and she crooked a finger at him as she crawled backward on the bed, calling him forward.

"Then why don't you show me?"

She hoped she was sounding like the vixen she was trying so confidently to portray, but the truth was, she had no idea what she was doing.

She liked to think of herself as a sensual woman, but she was also still a young lady who, despite her lack of proper chaperoning, did not have the opportunities nor the inclination to seek out gentlemen and be the wanton, worldly woman she would be were her life circumstances different.

But at this moment, with Gideon standing before her, she craved a taste of that forbidden fruit. His piercing gaze held an intensity that sent shivers down her spine, awakening dormant desires that she had imagined but, she realized now, never could have properly understood. He closed the distance between them, drawing over top of her, his hand reaching out to brush against her cheek.

Madeline's heart raced in anticipation as she nuzzled her cheek into the strength of his hand, heat radiating from his body to hers, his scent enveloping her senses with notes of sandalwood and musk blending in a heady cocktail that intoxicated her further. Her fingers trembled slightly as she untied her wrapper, allowing it to fall to the sides and expose her nightdress.

Unlike that of most young women, it was not a virginal white gown that hid every bit of skin from her chin down to her toes, but rather a custom black silk that she had always enjoyed the feel of over her skin – and now, she hoped that Gideon could enjoy it too.

His eyes widened in what she could only describe as a surge of desire, as his inhale sounded more like a gasp. A flicker of uncertainty crossed his gaze, but it was gone nearly as quickly as it had arrived.

Gideon's hands trembled as he hovered above her, his gaze locked on her with an intensity that made her heart thud against her chest. Madeline could see the battle of longing and hesitation rage within him, but she refused to allow doubt to consume this moment – not from him, and certainly not from her.

With a flicker of confidence, she reached out and gently grasped his hand, guiding it to the edge of her nightdress. As his fingertips brushed against her exposed skin, a low growl rumbled from deep within his throat, throwing away any hesitation that might have been present and replacing it with a surge of instinct instead.

When he slipped the straps off her shoulders, Madeline arched her back, allowing the fabric of her nightdress to slide down her body, revealing the curve of her breasts and the swell of her hips. She watched as Gideon's gaze traced every inch of her exposed skin.

"You are beautiful," he murmured, and Madeline's heart leapt at the praise. She was no beauty, she knew that – her features were too prominent, her curves too round – but the fact that Gideon was taken enough with her to say so meant more to her than a flirtatious comment from any other man ever could.

She knew him. He wasn't a man who would say something that he did not wholeheartedly believe.

Leaning down, he pressed his lips against the delicate skin of her neck, leaving a trail of fiery kisses along her collarbone and down the center of her chest. The sensation of his warm breath against her skin intensified the ache between her thighs.

"Do you know what you are doing to me?" she said huskily, causing him to chuckle softly.

"I may have an idea."

Gideon's lips trailed lower, teasingly grazing over the swell of her breasts before he took one tender nipple into his mouth, suckling gently. A moan escaped Madeline's lips as pleasure coursed through her. Her fingers tangled in Gideon's hair, urging him closer, desperate for more.

He obliged, his tongue swirling around her sensitive flesh, alternating between gentle licks and teasing flicks. Each caress sent the blood pumping harder through Madeline's veins, her body writhing beneath him, craving release.

But Gideon had other plans in mind. He continued his exploration downward, leaving a trail of kisses along the curve of her stomach until he reached the junction of her thighs. Madeline swallowed hard as his warm breath brushed against her most intimate area and she opened herself, wondering if now was the moment in which they would join together. What would it be like? She knew it might hurt, and yet, from what her friends had told her, it was far more pleasurable than painful.

She believed them, if this was any indication.

Gideon's hands gently held her hips, keeping her steady as he positioned himself between her legs. Madeline's entire body buzzed with desire and need, the ache within her growing almost unbearable. She tangled her fingers in the sheets beneath her, desperate for something to hold onto.

"Gideon," she panted. "I want... I need... more."

"More is coming," he said gruffly, and then, with deliberate slowness that made Madeline whimper in anticipation, his tongue made contact with her folds.

She let out a cry, about to ask him what he was doing, to tell him that this was too much, that he needed to stop, but then a surge of delight shot through her body, making her back arch off the bed. He started with soft, teasing licks, gradually increasing the pressure and intensity until she was becoming frantic beneath him.

Madeline's sighs turned into moans as Gideon expertly explored every inch of her core. She figured that most women would be embarrassed, but the thought quickly fled as his tongue danced across her sensitive flesh, finding every sweet spot and making her tremble. Each stroke of his tongue sent shivers down her spine, threatening to unravel her very being.

Her fingers clenched and unclenched in the sheets as Gideon's lips locked around her swollen bud, sucking gently yet insistently. The sensation was overwhelming, driving her closer to the edge. Madeline's breathing grew ragged, and her body tensed with anticipation. She was teetering on the precipice, yearning to fall into the abyss that awaited her.

Gideon must have sensed her nearing climax and shifted his focus. As his tongue continued to tease her, he slid two fingers inside of her, crooking them forward, somehow knowing exactly what she had been needing. The combination of his expert movements and the rhythm of his ministrations pushed Madeline beyond the brink. Wave after wave of pleasure crashed over her like the tempestuous sea, until she could do nothing but collapse back into the bed, completely sated.

She had thought she didn't like when Gideon tried to control those around him, but she found in this... she didn't entirely mind. Gideon Sutcliffe was most certainly a surprise.

But a surprise in the very best way.

CHAPTER 14

Gideon couldn't help but grin proudly in satisfaction as he pushed himself up onto his hands and knees and stared down at Madeline lying back, hair fanned around her head, her eyes closed, her arms splayed out to the side.

"Madeline," he whispered, trailing a finger down her cheek, "are you well?"

For a moment, she didn't move and he wondered if she had fallen asleep. But then the corner of her lip quirked upward and her eyes opened slightly.

"I am not certain," she said with an abashed smile. "After what you just did to me, it seems that I can barely move."

"Then my job is done," he said, sinking to the bed and lying beside her. He was still somewhat in awe that she had welcomed him like this, had wanted him over other men she could have had. "Thank you."

She raised her brows, turning her head to look at him. "I am fairly certain that I should be the one thanking you." She looked down for a moment, the oddest glimmer of shyness crossing her face. "I thought I had learned quite a bit from my books, but I wasn't aware that... *that* was possible."

Gideon's chest swelled at the idea that he was the one to have taught her of such a thing.

"I do know, however... what comes next," she continued.

Those words, in her husky voice, had his cock twitching, but he had to rein in his desires as he turned over to look at her.

"That's not going to be happening."

Her eyes flew to his. "Why not?"

"I told you that I wouldn't ruin you."

"I told you that I would only be ruined if I decided so."

Gideon leaned over and smoothed his hand down the side of her face, hoping he could ease the tension that filled it.

"I am not saying I do not want to... be with you in that way," he said, "for I most assuredly do. But I am not the man who will take a young woman's innocence when he might not have the ability to marry her."

"Who said I would marry you?"

Gideon couldn't help but chuckle at her inability to give in, even when there was no true argument to be had. He had avoided her in the past because he was scared of what might come out of her mouth – who would ever have thought there would come a day when he couldn't wait to hear the next thing she would say.

"That is true, you never agreed. But rest assured, Madeline, if the opportunity presents itself, then you can expect the question, and not just because of what has happened here between us tonight."

She was silent for a moment, her expression unreadable, but instead of answering she leaned over and began to trail her hand down his bare chest, stopping at the top of his breeches. Gideon swallowed, knowing that if she pushed

THE HEIR'S FORTUNE

him too hard, he just might not be able to deny her any longer.

"Madeline," he said, his voice gruff as he caught her hand. "What are you doing?"

"Continuing this love play," she said flippantly. "It isn't fair for me to have all of the fun."

"I had fun," he said. "Trust me in that. We have taken this as far as it can go."

"Are you so sure about that?" she asked, untying his wrapper yet again, and he had to swallow hard.

"I do not expect anything from you," he said, shaking his head. "That was my gift. I—"

"I want this," she said fiercely. "I want to do this – with you." She paused, a little less self-assured. "I do not know entirely how, but I shall do my very best."

"I have no concern at your prowess," he said. "But if you do not feel comfortable, stop at any time."

"I have a feeling that you will not be saying that again," she said with a coy grin before she lowered herself down, and he noted with some surprise that he was completely exposed before her now.

He was already hard for her, pulsating with his need, as Madeline's hand grazed his length. Gideon's breath hitched, his body responding eagerly to her touch even as he tried to hold back from giving himself completely over, not wanting this to end too soon. The intensity of the moment hung in the air, thick with anticipation.

Madeline's lips curled into a mischievous smile as she leaned in closer, her warm breath fanning against his skin. Slowly, tantalizingly, she pressed a gentle kiss to the tip of his member, eliciting a shiver that coursed through his entire body. Gideon's grip tightened on the sheets beneath him as he fought to maintain control.

She was not the first woman he had ever been with. But

she was the first who meant more to him than a quick moment of pleasure.

Her touch grew bolder, her tongue swirling around his sensitive flesh, teasing and exploring every inch of him, each caress sending him deeper into Madeline's spell. He surrendered himself to the sensation, allowing Madeline to take him further than he had ever allowed himself before.

Her mouth enveloped him fully, her lips sliding down his length with a steady rhythm that had Gideon's head spinning. The way she moved, her breasts bobbing over top of him, the passion behind every stroke of her tongue, made it impossible for him to suppress his groans. He arched his back, leaning forward and lacing his fingers into her hair as she worked her magic.

She became more fervent, her mouth working wonders on his member. Anything she lacked in experience, she more than made up for with enthusiasm. She seemed to know exactly what he needed, taking him to the edge only to pull back at the last moment, prolonging the sweet torment. Gideon's hips bucked involuntarily, seeking more of her intoxicating touch as he began to unravel beneath her as he lost himself in the sensation, forgetting everything else but the woman who held him in her hands.

Time seemed to stretch as he finally gave himself over and fell. His release came with a rush, consuming him as he cried out Madeline's name.

Madeline held onto him tightly, her hands supporting him through the aftershocks of his orgasm. As his breathing steadied, Gideon slowly opened his eyes and found himself entranced by the sight before him. Madeline's face was flushed, her eyes sparkling with a mix of satisfaction and mischief.

"Have you bewitched me?" he asked in wonderment as she gently withdrew from him, rocking back on her heels.

THE HEIR'S FORTUNE

Gideon laced his hands into his hair and tried to catch his breath.

Madeline threw herself forward, stretching out beside him, and he lifted one hand and placed it on her side, the only thing he had the energy to do at the moment.

"Was that... all right?" she asked, clearly trying not to show how much his response mattered.

"All right?" he repeated in disbelief, turning his head to the side to look at her. "That was incredible."

She smiled then and burrowed forward toward him, her head fitting perfectly into the crook of his neck between his head and his shoulders.

Just a week ago, he couldn't stand this woman.

Now, she was appearing more and more perfect for the life he was building.

Perhaps he could turn this moment into forever.

All he had to do was find that damn treasure.

* * *

Madeline rose in confusion the next morning. A few quick yaps sounded from somewhere beyond the bed and she rubbed her eyes, trying to determine what the noise was.

The sun was on her face, trying to find a way through her eyelids, which was nothing new. She had never been one to enjoy rising early.

But when she flung her arms out to the side, it was not the empty yet well-cushioned bed she was used to. Instead, it was a hard, warm chest that she encountered.

"Gideon!" she exclaimed, her eyes flying open as all that had occurred the night before came rushing back. She was still in some disbelief and also rather excited to do it again.

But that would have to wait.

Gideon sat up even quicker than she had, rubbing the sleep out of his eyes as he looked from one side to the other.

"My God, it's morning," he said, quickly scrambling out of bed, rousing Scout, who began to jump around him excitedly once he realized what time it must be. "My valet will be here soon."

His bedroom did not look quite as opulent in the light of day. The curtains were more faded than Madeline had realized, the wood more scarred, the marble around the fireplace more chipped.

And yet, it still held a certain charm, just like the rest of Castleton did.

She had no judgment for it – her own home was far from grand and just hanging together due to what was entailed – but she knew what it meant to the Sutcliffe family.

"Who is that?" she asked, pointing to the painting across from them. "I forgot about him last night but now in the light of day I feel as though he is watching me."

"That is my great-grandfather," he said.

"The one who was married to your Spanish great-grandmother?"

"That's the one," he said. "He was quite the adventurer."

He said it wistfully, as though he wished he were the same.

"Well, he is the only one who will know our secret," she said with a shrug, not quite as concerned as Gideon seemed to be. But then, Gideon had always been one to play by the rules.

"Your father entrusted my mother to be your chaperone while you are in residence," he said as he hurriedly pulled his wrapper around himself and found her clothing, ever the gentleman as he lifted her nightclothes from the floor and began to help her dress. "If she found out where you had spent the night, she would feel obliged to not only inform him but also ensure that I did right by you. Which I would like to, but—"

He stopped, discomfort on his face, and she smiled grimly and finished for him, "But you might have to marry another."

All of the warmth of the night that had enveloped her suddenly fled with the cold truth of the morning.

"You know that if I had any choice in the matter, Madeline, it would not be this way," he said, and she wished that he was saying something else – anything else – for she rather enjoyed how adorable he looked with his normally polished hair dishevelled and his wrapper tied so askew.

"I understand, Gideon. You have made the reasons for your decisions abundantly clear," she said as she finished tying her own wrapper and strode toward the door, stopping with her hand upon the knob. "However, if who you marry is not your choice… then just whose is it?"

And with that, she petted Scout, opened the door, and strode out, determined not to look behind her.

CHAPTER 15

"Oh, Gideon!"

Gideon looked up from his desk, upon which he had spread out the painting that had proven to be a map of Castleton. He was holding the ocular device to his eye, looking through it at the map once more to ensure that he knew exactly where to begin this time.

But his sister interrupted him.

"Gideon, why are you looking at that map again?" she asked from the doorway, where she stood with baby Jack in her arms. Scout left his pillow at Gideon's side and walked over to them but sat in front of them respectfully, his tail waving back and forth excitedly. "You know exactly where you are to go. Now all we need to do is search again, once everyone arrives and we are able to ensure our safety."

"I want to be certain," he said, not wanting to tell her that the stakes of finding the treasure had risen significantly – for him, at least.

"Will you watch Jack for an hour or so?"

Gideon started, for this was not a usual request. "Where are you going?"

"Devon and I must do something."

He rolled his eyes. "I do not want to know anymore."

"I never said what we were doing."

"Where is the nanny?" he asked as he began to roll up the map before tucking it away in its container and locking it back in the desk where he knew it would be safe.

"Today is her one afternoon off."

"Where is Mother?"

"With Father. They are on their ride."

"I hope someone is watching over them," he said, concerned that they would be out in the open when danger still lurked. He was becoming rather worried as it had been a few days since they had heard anything of Madeline's kidnappers.

"Yes. Anderson is with them, and they are staying on the grounds, close to the house."

He nodded.

"Is Madeline not here to help you with Jack?" he asked, trying to think of an escape from watching the baby. He loved his nephew, but he did not feel he had the skills required to keep a baby happy – even just for an hour. Cassandra had no time for his questions, however, as she sighed, placing her free hand on her hip.

"Gideon, I thought you might like to spend some time getting to know your nephew, but it seems I was mistaken. I will go find Madeline and see if she can help."

"Fine, fine," he said, waving her in, standing and holding out his hands tentatively. "This is all rather untoward."

"Well, I am rather untoward," she said with a smile. "I shall be back. Jack enjoys the back parlor."

Gideon held the baby out in front of him. Jack's lips turned up, and Gideon wondered whether it was an actual smile or if he made those expressions for everyone.

"Very well," he said with a sigh. "To the back parlor we go, as, apparently, that is your preference." He turned to look at Scout, who stood to follow along. "What do you think, Scout? Do *you* like the back parlor?"

He was still shaking his head once they made it to the parlor, wondering how a baby could enjoy one room over the other, when he came to a complete stop, inwardly cursing his sister for he suddenly had a feeling that she had known exactly what she was doing.

"Madeline, what a surprise," he said wryly, wondering how much she had told Cassandra about last night.

Madeline dropped her feet from the overstuffed blue Chesterfield to the floor as though she were a child who had been caught in mischief, her book falling from her hands as she rather comically tried to stuff it between the sofa and the cushion. Gideon wished he could read the title.

"Gideon, is that a baby in your arms?"

"It is," he said, suddenly relieved that she was here despite how they had left things. At least she would likely know what to do with the child. Her presence still disconcerted him after her parting comment that morning, and he didn't know how to make her understand the position he was in.

"What do I do with him?" he asked her as the dog jumped on the Chesterfield and curled up beside Madeline, dropping his head on her lap and looking up at her adoringly. Gideon was rather jealous of his position but he was far too occupied with the baby.

Gideon had always assumed he would be a father but had never considered what that would actually be like. Madeline laughed slightly as she gently moved Scout, stood, and walked over to them.

"He seems a little sleepy. Try placing his tummy against your shoulder and rocking with him back and forth."

Gideon tried, but he knew he was far too stiff and soon enough the baby began to wriggle and whimper slightly.

"Why do you not do it?," he said, holding him out to her, and Madeline stood with her arms out. The moment she took Jack, the baby settled against her shoulder and sighed contentedly before closing his eyes. Gideon stared at her in awe, both not understanding how a baby could sense the difference in the person holding him, and disconcerted at how Madeline with a baby was affecting him. She was much more motherly than he had imagined, and he was struck with images of her holding another baby – his baby.

"Do you like children?" he asked suddenly, and she scrutinized him with a brow raised.

"I did come here to help your sister with her baby."

"I know, but I was uncertain if you would ever be interested in having children of your own."

"Is that not what women of my standing are good for?"

He heard the sarcasm in her tone and lifted a shoulder. "I suppose that is why I wondered. You seem like a woman who wants more of life than being someone's wife."

"Can I not be someone's wife and also be more?" she asked. "Men are someone's husband and yet are still lauded for their accomplishments. Besides, I do not ask for much. I would like to be a mother, yes, if God wills it. I would also like to continue to ride my horses and—"

She stopped abruptly.

"And?" he said probingly. "You can tell me."

"I would like to spend more time *training* horses," she said shyly. "I love working with them, learning to understand the bond between human and horse and have them respond to me. Yet all of my horses have been trained by others before they are given to me to ride. I know my father did that out of safety, for no one would give a green horse to a lady, and yet, I would so dearly love to be the one to be there from the beginning."

Gideon reached over and placed a hand on her knee. "If…

if we find the treasure and it is, indeed, a fortune, then I will make sure that your dream comes true."

She scoffed as she shook her head. "Do not make promises that you cannot keep."

"I am not," he said with a shrug. "I said *if* we find the treasure."

"If," she said, shaking her head. "If, if, if. That damn treasure."

"That damn treasure," he said, his voice rising slightly, "is what could make all of the difference in our lives."

"Because you and I are not enough," she said, her voice matching his.

"I wish we were!" he countered. "I wish with everything within me. But it is not just me, Madeline. If I wanted to be selfish, I would marry you and to hell with the rest of it. But people rely on me. Servants, tenants, and the people in the village. Others in the *ton* might believe that my family has suffered by not having the fortune we used to. But my family has been just fine. We can survive with tired furniture and wilted vegetables. When we cannot afford to pay the village blacksmiths, or hire more maids, or provide for groundskeepers and gamekeepers, however, that means that all of those people who should be in those positions are the ones who suffer. For then they cannot even put food on their tables."

He finished, breathing heavily, and Madeline stared at him, stunned.

She had never considered all of that. She had only seen what he had pointed out, the obvious, the things that all of the *ton* gossiped about. She had been a fool, and as selfish as he had explained he could have been.

"I'm sorry, Gideon," she said, standing with the baby in her arms. Jack began to cry slightly, apparently sensing her

THE HEIR'S FORTUNE

discord, which in turn sparked Scout to whine. "I never thought of all of that."

He ran a hand through his hair.

"I was rather harsh. I apologize as well. I suppose I am rather... disconcerted if I am being honest with you."

"Why, Gideon, were you overcome with all that occurred last night?"

He chuckled as he watched her rock back and forth, swaying her hips from side to side as Jack cuddled into her shoulder.

"Something like that."

"You seemed rather adept at what you were doing," she said with a mischievous grin and Gideon's cheeks heated.

"Adept, yes," he said. "Affected... also yes."

She only smiled as she began humming a tune and continued her walk around the room, and Gideon wished his heart wasn't pounding quite so hard at the reminder of their night together.

"Once everyone else arrives, we will search for the treasure, will we not?" she asked over her shoulder, and he nodded.

"Yes. Then we will know... what is to come."

She turned around, her dark eyes piercing into his, saying so much more than their words could. Gideon had told her more of his inner thoughts than he ever shared with anyone, but it was the only way he knew to try to help her understand.

"So we will."

They were both silent for a moment, considering the implications of what that could mean.

"I heard from the magistrate in Colchester," Gideon said, changing the subject. "It seems that *Don* Rafael was released, after all."

Madeline's jaw dropped.

"Why?"

"It was as you said," Gideon admitted bitterly. "He was a nobleman from Spain. To keep him in English custody would only sour what are already strained relations. He was seen to a ship and promised to return to Spain."

"But you do not believe he did."

"Of course not. If he was willing to attempt to kill English nobility, then he certainly would not abandon his quest. Not when he is this close. He may not have appeared here himself, but I know he was behind it all."

"So how do we find him?" Madeline asked from over the sleeping baby's head, holding him close against her chest as though she could protect him from all that the world had in store.

"We don't," Gideon said grimly. "He will find us."

* * *

"So?" Cassandra said, peeking her head in the door of the parlor a short time later. "How was Jack?"

"An angel, like always," Madeline said softly from where she lay back on the Chesterfield once more, only this time she had a baby in her arms instead of one of her scandalous books. She didn't turn her body toward Cassandra for fear of waking the baby, but she did try to shift her gaze toward her. "I know what you did."

"Oh?" Cassandra said with an air of innocence as she walked through the room and sat on the matching chair. "And what is that?"

"You were trying to bring me and Gideon together," Madeline accused her, although without malice. She hadn't shared with Cassandra what had happened between them. She and Cassandra usually told one another everything, but this was Cassandra's brother. It hardly seemed like something that should be shared. She also didn't need another person devastated if this didn't work out.

"And, did it work?" Cassandra said hopefully, and Madeline sighed, stroking her hand over the soft hair on Jack's head.

"I will not lie to you, Cassandra. I do feel something for Gideon."

Cassandra leaned forward eagerly at the news and waited for Madeline to continue.

"I am hesitant to pursue it, however."

"Whyever not? I know that Gideon can sometimes be a little prudish, but—"

Madeline bit her lip, hoping Cassandra wouldn't see the blush that was stealing up her cheeks.

"It is not that," she said. "At first, to be honest with you, it was due to knowing about how he sent you away."

"Oh, Madeline, we have spoken about that—"

"I know," Madeline said, "and I do have a better understanding of what happened now and that he thought he was doing the right thing but listened to the wrong people. Now I am uncertain since Gideon might have to pursue another woman. One with a more significant dowry."

"That is rubbish," Cassandra said, waving a hand in the air as though pushing away the idea. "He is doing a fine job rebuilding the dukedom as it is. Yes, the progress is slow, but eventually, he will get there, with or without a dowry to assist him."

"Perhaps, but he does not think it will happen fast enough," Madeline said with a sigh. "He is worried about all of the people without employment, all of the people in the village and tenants on the land. His hopes have been resting in this treasure, but if it comes to naught, then this is his secondary plan. I wish I could help him, but it would be slow progress and I would never want him to live in guilt or to resent me."

"Well, then," Cassandra said, standing with her hands on her hips, "we will just have to make sure the first plan works out so that he doesn't have to do something stupid."

She began to stride out of the room, likely to tell Gideon exactly what she thought.

"Cassandra?" Madeline hissed as loudly as she could.

"Yes?" Cassandra said, stopping in the entrance.

"I really am famished. Will you take the baby?"

"Oh, yes!" Cassandra said as though she had forgotten him. "Of course."

She plucked Jack from Madeline's arms and hurried out of the room, not swayed from her purpose.

When Cassandra had her mind set on something, there was no stopping her.

And for once, Madeline was glad of it.

CHAPTER 16

"You're back," Gideon said, turning to look over his shoulder when he heard the footsteps on the terrace behind him, finding his sister waiting for him once more. "Does Jack need watching again?"

"No," she said, even though they both knew that wasn't why she was there. "It is about something Madeline told me."

"Cassandra, while I appreciate your interest in seeing me happy, I am perfectly capable of seeing to my own life."

"Sometimes you need a little help."

"Not this again," he said with a sigh, turning away from the view before him – a view that simply reminded of how much work needed to be done to return his property to its former glory. "I wish you and Devon would stop seeing me as a man who cannot fend for himself."

"That is not all, Gideon," she said, rounding to stand in front of him so that he could no longer see the grounds. "It is that I know you, and you will always do what you feel is best for others and not think about yourself so we have to do that for you. What is this nonsense about marrying for a dowry?"

"It's not nonsense," he said, crossing his arms over his chest in defense of himself. "It might, practically, be the only option."

"You know, Gideon, Madeline was a great help to her father in making decisions on his estate."

Gideon knew that Cassandra was just trying to help, but she was only making things worse.

"I'm sure she would be a great asset, Cassandra, but that would not be why I would choose to have her in my life. This is my responsibility. Besides that, rebuilding the estate will take some time. Time which I am not sure that we have."

"They have waited this long," she countered.

"It has been too long already."

"So it has. But everyone is making do, and people support you, Gideon, truly they do. Everyone, from the servants to the tenants, knows what you have been faced with and what you are trying to do."

"And I am failing."

"You are not." She stepped closer, that determined expression that he knew well covering her face as she lifted a finger and pointed it at him. "Believe that you are enough, Gideon. And if you forget, well, that's why I am here to remind you."

He sighed as she turned on her heel and walked away. He looked down at Scout, who was studying him quizzically as one ear flopped down low.

"I know. I should say something," he muttered before calling out, "Cassandra?"

"Yes?" she said, turning around and taking a few steps back toward him.

"I just want you to know that I do... I appreciate you. All you have done for me and are still doing. Especially—"

She grinned at his inability to express himself properly.

"I know, Gideon. I love you too." And with a spring in her step, she turned and walked away.

* * *

"They're here!"

As Cassandra with Jack and Madeline with Scout hurried to the front window, Gideon held back, his hands in his pockets as he waited for his friends' arrival. Once they were here, their plan would begin to take place. He wasn't nearly as excited as he had been before, for he knew now that there was far too great a chance that something could get in his way and halt this before it even began.

But once they all arrived, it would, in one way or another, be the beginning of the rest of his life.

Whether that journey was a smooth road or a treacherous one remained to be seen.

"Whitehall, good to see you," he said, shaking the viscount's hand as he and his wife, the former Lady Hope, walked through the front door. They lived the closest to Castleton so it made sense that they would arrive first, although Gideon knew they had already taken extensive travels over the past year.

It would take longer for Hope's sister, Faith, and her husband, Lord Ferrington, to journey to Castleton, for they lived a good deal farther and had just returned home a few weeks ago. Although Ferrington was always up for adventure, so it likely didn't take much to have him back in his carriage once more.

Rowley – Ferrington's brother – and his wife, whom all of the women affectionately called Percy, would likely beat them here as they were travelling from London, where he was working on his research.

Here Gideon was, disrupting all of their lives once more.

He knew they wanted to help, but he also hated that they likely saw him as a chump who they had to continually leave the rest of their lives behind for. Did Madeline feel that way too?

"Who is this?" Whitehall asked, bending down, surprising Gideon by showing attention to the dog, who jumped up and licked his face.

"Scout," Gideon said. "We found him on the property and he's decided to make himself at home here."

At that moment, Madeline looked across the room and caught his eye, and suddenly it seemed as though Scout belonged to both of them. Which would make it difficult if she eventually had to leave.

The women followed Hope upstairs, likely to discuss all that had occurred and Gideon did his duties as host, even though he couldn't help but wish that this was all over – and he could know whether he had a chance with the woman he was falling in love with.

* * *

The rain was falling softly the next morning – which was exactly as Madeline preferred it. She knew that she likely shouldn't be out riding alone, not with everything that had happened to her, but she was confident enough on a horse that she knew no one could be a threat as she rode. One thing she could say for her father was he had always found the best mount for her.

Victor, the stable hand, was less than thrilled that she was alone, making his opinion known with frowns and continual comments about the weather.

"It is really raining, my lady," he said. "You will be soaked."

"I like the rain," she said with a smile, although he still seemed dubious. "It is freeing."

He nodded, although from his expression she had the feeling that he thought she was out of her mind.

Her horse whinnied at her when they stepped outside the stables, but after a toss of her head, continued on, used to Madeline taking her out in all kinds of weather. Madeline knew Lady – she would rather be out here running in the rain than cooped up in the stables, much like her.

She led her to the field where she and Gideon had raced before, giving her the lead to run as she wished. It was tranquil out here, the air filled with a subtle mist, the rain not pouring any longer but rather descending gracefully from the heavens.

The grass below her horse's feet took on a deeper shade of green, the scent of the wet earth rising around them.

And, for now at least, she was alone, not a figure to be seen around her.

Gideon had told her last night that the horses they had recovered had, indeed, belonged to a stable near the coast and they would be sending servants to return them to where they belonged. No word had been heard about her captors since, and the cabin where they had kept her had been cleared out.

It made her wonder just where they could be now, but this was not why she was out here. She was trying to clear her mind, not fill it with anxious thoughts.

When she turned around to return to the house, breathing heavily from her sprint, she started in surprise at the rider who appeared in the distance. She paused, her heart pounding at the thought of who it could be until she noted the way the man moved, the tilt of his head and the size of his horse. Her pulse began racing for an altogether different reason.

Gideon.

She hadn't risked returning to his bedroom last night, nor had he appeared at her door. It seemed that they had come to an unspoken agreement that they would wait to see whether there was a chance for them before they continued to become closer, for otherwise, it might only lead to heartbreak. It had taken years for Madeline to open her heart to a man, and now that she finally had, there was an equally good chance that they could never finish what they had started.

She and Gideon rode toward one another, each at the same speed, a quick trot, until they drew their horses next to one another. Neither of them said a word but rather held each other's gaze, slow and serious.

"Do you always ride in the rain?" he finally asked, water slowly dripping off the brim of his hat.

"I do," she said. "Do you?"

"Not usually," he said. "Only when I am chasing a woman who insists on running from me."

"I am not running from you," she said. "When I saw you... I ran *to* you."

"So you did," he said, reaching out a hand and catching hers within it. The rain had soaked her glove to her skin, and his hand warmed hers through.

"Madeline," he said, drawing her as close as their horses would allow. "Whatever happens, I need you to know something."

She waited.

"I am falling in love with you."

Madeline felt the tears begin to well in her eyes, and as they started to fall, she hoped he wouldn't notice but rather would simply think that they were part of the moisture from the sky.

"Don't say that," she whispered.

"It's the truth," he said simply with a shrug. "A truth you needed to know."

"Why are you telling me this now?" she asked, trying to keep her breathing steady and even.

"In case I don't get the chance later. I know I am making a

mess of things, but even if we cannot be together, you deserve to know that you are worthy of love, that you deserve a man who can give you the world."

"Are you sure—" she began, but choked off her words with a sob.

"Sure of what?"

"That it is not just that I am simply the last option? Everyone is arriving, and they are all in pairs, married off, but me. I—"

"Madeline," he said, his voice almost harsh. "I am not saying this to boast, but only because you need to understand the truth. I will be a duke one day, and as much scandal is attached to this family's name, the title still goes a very long way. I could have nearly any woman that I choose, but if I am given the choice – I will choose you."

Her legs were facing his way in the saddle, and it didn't take much to slide off her horse and move to his lap. Her leap was not graceful nor was her seat comfortable, but he didn't seem to mind as his arms came around her to hold her up tightly. She leaned in, her lips descending on his, and he kissed her back with all of the passion that had been in his words.

He had questioned her decision to ride in the rain, but he hadn't chastised her, hadn't told her that she was being foolish. He respected her, and he… well, apparently, he was falling in love with her.

It was more than Madeline could ever have hoped for, and yet, she was reluctant. For happy endings never worked out for her. It was why she always fought Cassandra on what made a true romance. Madeline felt that the happily ever afters Cassandra so enjoyed were not realistic, and it made no sense to count on them. Madeline had seen too many tragic endings.

This love story had all of the makings of a tragic gothic

novel as much as it did one of Cassandra's romances – so would she take the risk, or would she walk away before it was too late?

CHAPTER 17

The next day brought with it a flurry of arrivals, and the quiet country respite that Gideon had been enjoying was now a house party once again.

Although, as much as he hated to admit that he couldn't handle this himself, there was relief in having additional manpower to provide protection – or to perhaps even ward off any attacks.

They were currently sitting around the drawing room as he and Cassandra updated them on all that had occurred.

"It is rather hard to believe that this could all be over soon," Rowley said, pushing his glasses up his nose. "It seemed so simple when it began."

"With a riddle," Cassandra said with a smile.

"Leading to Anthony breaking the codes of the books," Hope added.

"With your help," Whitehall said, placing his hand on his wife's leg.

"Then there was our discovery of the necklace in Bath," Percy said with a smile at Rowley.

"Which turned out to not be a necklace at all, but a

compass and ocular device that helped us with the map we found in Spain," Faith finished, and Ferrington chuckled.

"Who would have thought that we would all have a hand in this?"

"I would say it's our greatest adventure so far," Devon said, and Cassandra intertwined her fingers in his.

"Or the greatest of love stories," she said, beaming at all of them around the room, although her happiness made Gideon's stomach twist, for not all of them had found such an ending.

"We haven't yet finished this adventure, though," he said. "Now it is time to find the treasure."

"When would you like to go?" Devon asked, although from the look in his eye, Gideon was sure he was already aware of just what he was thinking.

"We should not wait too long," Gideon said, looking around at the gentlemen. "Did you all bring your firearms?"

"I truly hope it does not come to that," Hope said fervently.

"Nor do I, but it is best to be prepared," Gideon said grimly. "Why do we not go tomorrow? It will give you all time to settle in and have a decent meal and sleep before we begin tomorrow. After we have breakfast, we will meet at the front entrance. From my readings on the map, we shouldn't need horses, but it might be slow going as we will need the compass to find the final location."

"Does everyone have walking boots?" Cassandra asked, looking around, and Gideon held his hand up as he looked at her with some exasperation.

"Cassandra, do we really need to have this conversation?"

"We are going with you, Gideon, whether you like it or not," she said stubbornly. "We have all been a part of this as much as you have, and we are not going to sit here and darn socks while we wait for you to return!"

"I cannot say I have ever seen you darn a sock."

"You know what I mean," she said, continuing around him. "No one has heard anything of the Spaniards for days and we are likely safer with you than here alone. Either we accompany you or follow behind you. Your choice."

Gideon sighed as he looked around at the rest of the men, but they all just shrugged, none of them willing to take on the women.

"Very well," he said. "We shall go together."

* * *

"Here we thought we would not be seeing one another for ages, and we are back together already!" Percy said as the five women sat in a small circle in the drawing room after dinner.

"It is so different from the last time, though, is it not?" Hope said as she lifted her glass of brandy to her lips. Even though all of the men were now well aware of their secret appreciation for the drink, at this point it seemed tradition to enjoy it without them. "At our last party, we were all accompanied by chaperones, and here we all are, married women." Suddenly she stopped, a gasp escaping her lips as her eyelids flew up. "I am so sorry, Madeline, I should not have said that. I only meant that we do not have chaperones because we had to travel with one before we were married, and—"

"It is fine," Madeline said, waving Hope's worries away. "It is no insult. You are all happily married, and I am pleased for all of you."

"You will be soon as well, I am sure of it," Hope, ever the optimist, said enthusiastically.

Madeline reached across the table between them and patted her hand.

"You are kind, Hope, but I am not sure that is at all true."

"Are you certain about that?" Cassandra asked smugly from her seat next to Hope, raising one eyebrow from over her drink. "No gentleman has caught your eye as of late?"

Madeline glared at her, but of course, that only brought further attention to the subject.

"A gentleman?" Faith said, sitting up tall in surprise as she blinked at Madeline. "But you have been here at Castleton, have you not, after arriving from your father's country home? You haven't been to London for a great deal of time, so who would you—oh. Oh!"

Madeline sighed as realization slowly began to dawn upon all of them.

"Lord Ashford?" Percy said, a grin spreading across her face. "Oh, Madeline, how wonderful! You and Cassandra could be sisters-in-law, and you would live here at Castleton, which is not so far from some of us. Can you imagine, becoming a duchess one day?"

Madeline was holding up a hand, shaking her head and unable to help her wry laugh at how far ahead of themselves the women had gotten.

"You are all too excited about this. Cassandra said a gentleman might have caught my eye, and in that, she is correct. I have... *noticed* Lord Ashford, much more than I used to, now that a few misconceptions have been resolved."

Cassandra had never fully shared the circumstances of how or when she had been sent away with anyone but Madeline. As far as everyone else was concerned, she had gone to stay with relatives for a time.

Faith was slightly frowning, and Madeline turned to her, interested in what had agitated her about the thought.

"What concerns you, Faith?"

"Nothing at all," Faith said, especially when Hope obviously knocked her knee into her sister's leg. "I suppose I just never pictured you with someone like Lord Ashford. But who am I to say, as I am now married to a man completely my opposite?"

Cassandra turned to Faith, her brow furrowed.

"I believe they are perfect for one another."

"Well, of course, for you would love to have Madeline as part of your family," Faith countered, never one to hide how she truly felt.

"That may be, but I also want what is best for her, and for Gideon," Cassandra said, passion behind her words. "And the truth is that Gideon does not need a simpering miss who will only follow orders and try to please him. He needs a strong woman who is not afraid to speak her mind and who can also help him to *feel* things."

Madeline shifted uncomfortably. "I am not exactly a romantic, Cassandra."

"Not in a happily-ever-after optimistic sense, no, but you follow your heart, Madeline, as much as you do your head. Gideon needs someone who can draw on that emotion, who can teach him what love is, who can show him that life isn't just about ledgers and that not everything is right and wrong or black and white but that there is a balance."

She paused.

"Think of how he and Devon have always been such good friends and yet they are so different from one another. He needed Devon in his life when he couldn't be the voice for himself. Devon was there to show him not to take life quite so seriously, to help him open up to other people and find some fun, at least at times when he could. Now I think that you would equally balance him out in ways that he needs."

"And me?" Madeline couldn't help but ask. "I do understand what you are saying, and I do not think you are wrong, although I had never framed it quite like that. But am I to spend the rest of my life showing Gideon who he could be when he needs to have a better understanding of the people around him?"

"He would show you that you are worthy of his love. He would give you everything you need and more. When Gideon loves someone, he loves them fiercely. He doesn't allow many in, but once you are part of his inner circle, you are never leaving. He will protect you with everything he is, and will provide you with family, and home."

Madeline kept her eyes focused on the amber liquid in her glass, for she was afraid that if she looked up, she wouldn't be able to hide the tears that were swimming in her eyes.

She liked the sound of Cassandra's words – far more than she likely should, especially after Gideon's confession in the field that very morning.

"What do I do if there is no treasure?" she asked, her voice just over a whisper as she looked around at her friends. "What if he needs to marry someone else who can be there to help restore the family's fortunes? Then I would just be tossed aside."

"Gideon feels that if there is no treasure, he will have to marry someone with a large dowry," Cassandra explained, to which Percy waved a hand.

"He might think that, but would it actually come to it? There are other ways."

"That is what I said, but Gideon is adamant and Madeline does not want him to ever resent her or his decision," Cassandra said, with a pitying look at Madeline.

She was aware that Cassandra only wanted what she thought was best, but she also wanted nothing to do with the sympathy that was being sent her way.

"There is only one thing to do," she said, sitting up straight and finishing off her glass before pasting a smile on her face and looking around at her friends. "We must finish this treasure hunt and move on."

* * *

Gideon didn't spend a lot of time in Castleton's billiards room. Perhaps it was because he had far too much else to do. Perhaps it was because he didn't particularly like billiards. Or it could have been because the room was a setting from the 1700s. At one point in time, it had been rather opulent, with the large, ornate billiards table, burgundy and green tapestries and rugs, and elegant chandeliers.

Now, however, the leather-upholstered chairs and sofas were cracked, the surface of the billiards table showing its use, and the tapestries faded by sun.

But it provided a fine place for the five of them to be alone, and he needed to make sure that his friends understood the importance of their task tomorrow.

He stood in front of them, leaning back against the table behind him while they sat on chairs and the sofa that had been pushed against the wall.

"I know that we have undertaken a great many adventures before," he began. "But this is, perhaps, the most important. Not because of what the treasure might mean to me, but because of how high the stakes are. We all know that danger has been met upon this quest before, and of primary importance is to keep the women safe."

"Do you think the Spaniards that captured Madeline will come after us again?" Devon asked.

"I would consider it to be a high probability," Gideon said. "Where have they been since Madeline and I returned? They must be waiting until we find the treasure."

"That is rather disconcerting, to think that they might be

nearby," Ferrington said. "Should we look for them, to try to find them before they find us?"

"No," Gideon said, shaking his head "I think we draw them out. It will save us time and I would rather fight them on my home land."

"What about this group of people that seems to be on our side?" Rowley asked. "Who are they and why are they doing this?"

"I wish I knew," Gideon said, "but I can only hope that will be revealed in time."

"Faith tried writing to Abello, the butler in San Sebastian who helped Faith and me escape," Ferrington said, crossing his arms and leaning back. "He knew who we were, as well as what we needed. There has to be a connection there."

"You have not received a response?" Gideon asked, and Ferrington shook his head.

"No. But it could take some time."

"Very well," Gideon said. "We will go ahead without knowing, for we cannot wait any longer. You all have lives to return to and I have taken up far too much of your time."

"We want to be part of this, Gideon," Devon said in a low voice. "We wouldn't be here otherwise."

Gideon nodded, not wanting any of them to see the emotion they were causing within him.

"Thank you," was all he said. "Now, who is up for a game?"

They all joined heartily, and as Gideon looked around the room, he appreciated all that he had before him.

Even if he didn't have the words to say it.

CHAPTER 18

Madeline was surprised at how on edge she was when they began their walk through the gardens the next morning. Were anyone to come upon them, they would likely think they were a country party out for a lovely walk on a pleasant day considering the lateness of autumn.

They would have no idea of their true purpose.

Gideon was at the front of the group, holding the compass before him.

"The path starts here," he explained as they stopped at the edge of the gardens. "Then we are to continue this way." He pointed to the right.

"This will take us toward the lake?" Devon asked as they walked, and Cassandra shook her head.

"We will near the lake, but this path will continue round the back of it and follow the river."

"And where does that go?" Whitehall asked.

"Eventually it leads to a clearing beyond the lake, where the water trickles down in a small waterfall. More of a pond. Then it continues to a neighboring property. I am not certain how far we will be going, although I am sure we will remain on our land."

"Is there anywhere that a treasure could be hidden?" Ferrington asked.

"Not that I am aware of, but one never knows," Gideon said as they continued.

The ten of them were quiet the rest of the way, the only sounds being the calls of the robins and finches, the rustling of the leaves in the wind and underfoot, and the very distant lowing of cows and sheep that carried from the fields beyond the woods that they walked through.

First, they walked past the ruins of the old house that had stood there years ago, where Cassandra and Devon had spent a great deal of time searching, although that had come to naught. Still, it had brought them closer together.

Next, they entered a second grove of trees, silence remaining. Madeline wondered if they were all beginning to sense the edge that she and Gideon carried.

They continued down the path, which was no longer created by man but rather tread through the grass by animals and people over the years, until Madeline heard the lapping of water against the shore. As they walked, eventually the couples all found themselves next to one another. Madeline wasn't sure if it was due to being the two unpaired or whether it was meant to be, but she found herself walking next to Gideon.

"Is that the lake I hear?" she murmured to him, and he nodded.

"The lake is behind us now. We will follow the river it is attached to if I understand the map correctly."

They continued around a few twisting turns until eventually, they emerged into a small clearing. In all her years visiting Castleton, Madeline had never visited this area, and she stopped so abruptly that Percy walked right into her.

"Ow," Percy said, rubbing her nose, but Madeline couldn't concentrate, for she was too busy turning from one side to the next.

"This is… unbelievable," she said. A wide river stretched out in front of them, the edge of the lake pouring into a tiny waterfall, allowing water to trickle downward. "I didn't even know this was here." She looked at Cassandra. "Why didn't you ever show me?"

Cassandra shrugged one shoulder. "I never came here much, and I always promised Gideon that I would keep this area his secret. Well, his and my father's. My father always used to love coming here. I think sometimes my mother still brings him."

"I understand," Madeline said quietly, knowing how private Gideon was, how much it must be a respite to have a place he could come and have to himself.

"This is where the map has led us," he said, dismissing all that Cassandra was sharing. "Now we must follow the compass."

He pulled it from his pocket, holding it up in front of him, and they all waited as they watched him, seemingly without breathing.

"This way," he said, nodding forward, and they all walked behind him, still in their pairs, Madeline just a few feet behind Gideon.

He stopped at the tree line, pausing and looking around.

"From the map, we are to continue straight through the trees."

"There is nothing behind here but the hill beyond," Cassandra said, and Gideon frowned, stepping forward, until he finally ducked underneath one of the tall trees.

"Where are you going?" Cassandra called out. "We have explored every inch of this land. You know there is nothing here."

"This is where it is leading us so there must be *something*. I just hope it is not another blood—er, beastly clue," Gideon said, although his voice was muffled. There was a pause. "Here it is!"

Madeline and Cassandra exchanged a look of surprise.

"Here *what* is?' Cassandra asked.

"I do not quite know what you would call this," he said as they all ducked underneath the trees one at a time, until they were lined up beside him, staring at the side of the hill – only, Gideon was right. There was something there. A small space in the otherwise flat surface.

"Is it a cave?" Ferrington asked.

"It does not appear to be so, for I doubt anyone could completely fit within it. Certainly not stand," Gideon said, frowning as he pushed forward, sticking his head and shoulders into the hole and looking around.

Madeline was trying to be patient, but she wished she could push Gideon out of the way to see what was within. She couldn't imagine what Cassandra was feeling.

"I think we can fit a few of us in there," he said, turning around. "We might not be able to stand, but there should be plenty of room." He paused, a look of indecision on his face before he turned toward his sister, who was waiting eagerly, nearly bouncing on her toes in excitement. "Cassandra, why do you not go first?"

"Me?" Cassandra said, although her eyes did not hide her clear excitement at the opportunity. "You are not worried that it might not be safe?"

"Of course I am worried that it might not be safe," he said with a bit of a sigh. "But there doesn't seem to be any space for anything – or anyone – to be hiding in there in wait for us, and I know how important this is to you. You started this. You might as well finish it."

She looked at him before taking his hand. "We started this together. Let's finish this together."

He nodded and provided her a step up in the palms of his interlaced hands so that she could shimmy her shoulders and the top of her hips through the hole. Gideon followed, and the rest of them waited.

Madeline knew they were all eager to know if there was treasure within, but they also knew that this was most important to brother and sister, and they should be the ones to discover whether this had come to anything. Madeline's nails were biting into her palms, she was so nervous about what they might find.

That's when they heard the shout.

* * *

Gideon and Cassandra had crawled forward together, Gideon allowing his sister to take the lead. There was just enough sunlight filtering through the hidden entrance for them to see a few feet in front of them, and as much as his instincts were telling him to go ahead and make sure all was safe, he knew that he needed to trust Cassandra.

She was as much a part of this as he was, and he had been holding her back for too long – Madeline had made that abundantly clear.

Cassandra had been able to stand into a half-crouch, and he followed along behind, but then she halted so abruptly that he ran into her and nearly knocked her over.

Shockingly, she didn't even comment on it.

"Gideon," she breathed, her head scanning from side to side. "We found it. We found it!"

Her voice had risen as she spoke before she turned around and gripped his arms, bouncing up and down on her toes as best she could in their limited space. His eyes widened as he stepped beside her to see what was awaiting them – large, old, wooden chests tucked into the back corner. From the dirt and dust that had accumulated on top of them, they had been undisturbed for some time. Gideon stepped forward, reverently stroking his fingers over the lid of the chest closest to them.

"What do you suppose is inside?" he asked, his voice so low that he was surprised when Cassandra answered him.

"There is only one way to find out, isn't there?" she said, crouching beside him. "Open a chest."

He slid his fingers around the latch, only to find that a padlock kept it shut.

"Check the next one," he told his sister, and she was silent for a moment.

"The same."

Gideon took a deep breath, trying to quell his growing annoyance that every step of this treasure hunt only brought more resistance.

"The key," Cassandra said suddenly, staring at him with her palms flat on one of the treasure chests. "The key that unlocked the necklace, the one that Hope found in the piano," she said. "Could it, perhaps, open the padlocks?"

He lifted one of the locks, holding it up to inspect it.

"I suppose it wouldn't hurt anything to try," he said.

"Well, let us go and get it, then," she said. "The treasure has waited this long. I am sure that it can wait a few more hours."

"No need," he said, already walking over to the chest. "I have it right here."

"You carry the key around with you?" she said, her mouth hanging open.

"Usually," he said. "This treasure hunt has brought us so many surprises that I like to be prepared."

"Of course you do," she murmured and he smiled

sardonically.

He reached beneath his cloak to his jacket, finding the key in his pocket next to the compass. He lifted the padlock, said a quick prayer, and then attempted the key.

It clicked.

He looked up, meeting Cassandra's eyes, before he slowly turned it and the padlock sprang open. He lifted up the lock, set it to the side, and then slid the chain through the hole before ever so slowly pushing the lid upward. Now that the moment was finally here, he wasn't sure if he actually wanted to see what was within or not, for it could change everything. He didn't know if he was ready for that.

"Oh. My."

Gideon hadn't even realized his eyes were closed until he heard Cassandra's voice behind him, and his eyes flew open, the sight causing him to gasp as well. For there within were thick, round coins of gold. He had no idea what they were worth or what country they belonged to, but the metal of the coins alone would be worth a fortune, let alone whatever the currency was. He reached a hand in and allowed the coins to cascade over his fingers.

Cassandra did the same before plucking a coin out of the pile and holding it up before her.

"Do you think the other chests contain the same?" she asked, and he shrugged.

"There is only one way to find out."

The same key worked on the padlocks of the other chests, and soon all four stood open, showcasing their coins, a few jewels, and fine goblets set in straw that had allowed them to survive its many journeys.

"Is everything all right in there?" Devon called from outside the cave entrance, and Cassandra rushed to the hole.

"More than all right," she said, before turning back to Gideon, her eyes shining. "Do you know what this means?"

He knew exactly what it meant – that his prayers had been answered. He was so overcome with gratitude and relief that he couldn't put what he was thinking into words. Everything that had been weighing on him was slowly lifting off his shoulders, but all he could truly consider was that this meant he could have the woman he loved.

For he was no longer just falling for her, but he loved her with all that he was.

He had what he needed to offer himself to her, to give her his name, to share his life, in the fashion that she deserved – if she would have him. The prospect nearly knocked him over.

He urged Cassandra forward, out of the cave, before encouraging Devon and the rest of their friends to take turns going to look for themselves. When Madeline emerged, she had eyes only for Gideon, as she took purposeful steps toward him.

"It's a fortune, is it not?" she said in hushed tones, slowly walking backward with him until they were on the other side of the tree line, hidden from view of their friends, except for their feet if anyone should truly take a good look for them.

"It is," he said with a nod, a grin that he was helpless to stop from widening across his face. "Enough that I most certainly do not need to marry for a dowry."

"What a relief," she said, her eyes searching his, "for I have none."

And with that, he leaned down and kissed her with all that he felt within but had never been able to put into words. His affection, his desire, his very being that yearned for her with a desperation that was becoming more difficult to contain with each passing day was released into the kiss.

But no more, he realized as his heart began to beat far more rapidly with anticipation.

No more.

CHAPTER 19

Madeline was having a difficult time keeping her eyes away from Gideon for the rest of the night.

They all ate and drank in celebration, the brandy strong enough that no one much noticed just how horrible the venison was cooked.

Gideon had attempted to speak to his father about what they had found, but he was not in the right frame of mind to hear it – at least, not from what Cassandra had said. Madeline hadn't had a chance to speak to Gideon yet.

And yet, she watched him. The smile, which before today had been nearly absent, was now fixed on his face as he made no effort to conceal his glances toward her.

She was shocked by how this discovery had lightened his countenance. The furrow in his brow had eased, his smile more readily lit his lips, and his shoulders dropped by inches.

Madeline had grown to love Gideon for who he was and why he felt he needed to do what he had to do, but this Gideon was a man she could see herself truly enjoying her time with.

She didn't need him to be one or the other. But she liked that there could be both sides of him.

She couldn't help her mind from racing forward to the possibilities of what this could mean.

"What do we do now?" Devon asked when there was a moment of relative silence.

"We, along with some of our more trusted servants, will take wagons out to the cave to collect the treasure," Gideon said. "Then I will have to consult with some experts to determine just what exactly is within it all and what I should do with it."

Devon looked from one side to the other to make sure that no one was listening before he leaned in. "Can you trust your servants not to say anything or take any of the treasure for themselves?"

"Any that are still in our employ are most loyal. Their families have been with us for generations," Gideon said. "I would trust them with my life and I will be providing them with some compensation for not only helping us but for staying with us through all the years when times were hard."

Madeline leaned against the column beside her as she watched Gideon. How had she not realized the generosity within him? It made him all the more attractive to her, knowing that he would consider the needs of his servants as much as he would himself and anyone else in the room.

"As for the rest of you," he said, lifting his glass, but Ferrington was already waving his words away.

"Do not even think of it," he said. "We want nothing more than the opportunity to see this through to the end and know that we played a part in it."

"How do you even know that I was going to say something like that?"

"Because we know you well," Whitehall said. "Keep your fortune, Ashford."

"The adventure was worth it," Ferrington added.

"I will do something for all of you," Gideon insisted. "I promise. At the very least, I will give you each a small piece of the treasure to remember all of this."

"As if we could ever forget," Percy said with a laugh. "This is something that we will remember forever."

Gideon looked over at Madeline, his eyes hard and glinting, his mouth in a firm line. "Forever."

Somehow that seemed like a promise. She just had to wait and see how he meant to fulfill it – or perhaps she would have to take this into her own hands and be the savior for the two of them.

* * *

A FEW HOURS LATER, the ten of them had done a remarkable job of making the brandy disappear, although Gideon had made sure to keep his portion to a couple of glasses, slowly nursing them. He couldn't help but note that Madeline had done the same, and he wondered if that was usual for her or if she had a reason for wanting a clear head.

"Let's play a game!" Cassandra called out just when Gideon had begun to consider going upstairs to bed. Whether he would go alone or not remained to be seen.

"Have we not had enough games?" he couldn't help but ask, catching the amused smile Madeline cast his way. He had sensed more than seen her watching him all evening, and he couldn't help but wonder if she could feel the same tension that he did – the wanting, the waiting, the wondering if this would all be leading to something now that the obstacle that had been present between them had been cleared.

When she drew close to him, her drink at her mouth, a

seductive smile playing behind it, however, he knew that she was as invested in this as he was.

"You do not enjoy games, Gideon?" she asked in a low voice for his ears alone, and he turned to her, giving in to the desire to tuck a loose strand of hair behind her ear, the tendril silky beneath his fingers.

"Depends on the game," he said huskily with a meaningful stare.

"Looks as though Gideon is playing a game of his own," Cassandra called out, and he turned to glare at her.

"Very well, Casandra," he said, baiting his sister. "What game would you like us all to play?"

"Blindman's Bluff, of course!" she said, and Gideon sighed, for he had always hated that game, especially when he was the one blindfolded.

"Not to worry," came Madeline's low whisper in his ear, "we shall make it fun."

That had his senses stirring, and soon enough Cassandra, due to the game being her idea, was blindfolded and ready to find the rest of the players.

Gideon had no care who his sister caught or how. He had another game of chase in mind.

As Cassandra began to call out, reaching in front of her to try to catch anyone foolish enough to be within reach – such as her husband, of course, who had no issues in being caught – Madeline began to back away. Gideon kept his eyes locked on her as he followed her through the room and into the front foyer beyond, uncaring if any of them noticed the two of them leaving together. By this point, the ten of them trusted one another enough to keep any secrets, and if this ended the way he wanted it to, it wouldn't much matter anyway.

Gideon had no idea where Madeline was going or what she wanted to do, but he knew that he wouldn't be able to

THE HEIR'S FORTUNE

help but follow her wherever she went and in whatever she wanted to do.

She crooked a finger at him as she stepped through the doorway, across the foyer, and into the small front parlor on the other side. It was a small room, hardly ever used, and the fire in the grate wasn't even lit despite the house party. The door was always kept closed as the absence of many servants meant one less room to attend to.

Gideon walked over to a side table and lit a few candles to provide some light, the hiss of the dust on the oft-unused candle wicks a reminder of how rarely they utilized many of Castleton's rooms out of necessity.

He might have to go to work to begin filling them, he supposed, as he turned to watch Madeline through hooded eyes.

"I do not think this is how we are supposed to play the game," he said, taking unhurried yet urgent steps toward her, reaching out a hand and running his fingertips down her arm. "I believe one person is supposed to be blindfolded."

Madeline reached out, surprising him when she unfastened his cravat and ran it through her fingers before standing on her toes and lifting it to his head.

"Then blindfolded you shall be."

"Are we not supposed to play with all of the others?" he asked.

"I like when I'm the only one here for you to catch," she said, and, once his eyes were covered, she leaned up and pressed her lips against his. After a moment of surprise, he reached a hand out until he found her and wrapped it around the base of her skull, holding her tight as he leaned in and kissed her back with even more passion, his tongue teasing through her lips as he stroked her mouth in a possessive love play.

Gideon could tell that as much as Madeline always

presented herself as unaffected, her pulse was racing beneath his fingertips as he leaned back, his lack of sight heightening his other senses as her warm breath on his cheek had him on edge.

She pressed her cheek into his hand and he splayed his fingers outward, holding the back of her head while his thumbs ran over her defined cheekbones, her slightly upturned nose, the bow of her plush lips.

It was not his first exploration of her, but he could never imagine a more intimate one.

The coolness of the air was in stark contrast to the warmth of her skin, the air thick with a heady mix of longing, blocking out the world that lay beyond the parlor door.

Gideon's hands left Madeline's face, roaming down her shoulders, delicately outlining her collarbones, tracing the curves of her bodice, waist, and hips, memorizing every inch of her that he didn't already know. She leaned into his caress, and he revelled in her trust in him. He realized that as long as she was with him, his fears for what was to come vanished. The only one that remained was the possible loss of her from his life.

Their kisses grew fervent now as his hands cupped her bottom, pulling her in close between his legs, not hiding just how much he wanted her.

He leaned back, his breath coming hard and fast.

"Madeline," he rasped, "I don't know why it took me so long to see you, but now that I have, I know that I can never go another day without you before me. I'm finally free to offer myself to you, and I want you to be mine, more than I have ever wanted anything before. Will you... will you have me?"

She stilled in his arms, and he worried for a moment that he had read this all wrong, that she didn't want as much from him as he did from her – but then her soft laugh erased all of his doubts.

"Of course, Gideon," she said. "I wanted you before you found the fortune and I want you now. I am only grateful that we now have a way forward."

He left her side only long enough to cross the room and ensure that the door was firmly shut and locked before he returned, taking her in his arms once more and moving her backward until they reached the sofa, although he didn't lay her down just yet.

He knew he should take her to a bedroom, to make love to her the proper way, but he honestly didn't think he could wait that long – and then there was all of their friends on the other side of the door who he had no wish to move through. They likely had a good idea of what was happening in here, but there would be no hiding it if they walked through them.

Madeline's warm hands came to his cheeks, pressing against them, her lips soft against his ear.

"Make love to me, Gideon," she whispered. "Make me yours."

It was a request that he could no longer deny.

CHAPTER 20

Madeline was being more brazen than most young women should be – but she had known Gideon long enough now to realize that she didn't scare him away.

At least, not anymore.

She sensed his pause, in which he was likely considering if this was the right thing to do, but after that brief moment, his lips crashed back down on hers, his intention clear. If the way he was currently making love to her mouth was any indication of how he would make love to her body, she wondered if she would truly be able to survive it.

The world around them seemed to melt away, leaving just the two of them, locked together in their passionate embrace. Her hands roamed his chest, over the hard muscle beneath his linen shirt and waistcoat, and he in turn explored every inch of her back and waist, tracing the line of her bodice with his fingers.

Madeline's heart raced as his lips travelled down her neck, leaving a trail of scorching kisses in their wake. She arched her back slightly, her breath catching in her throat as his fingers found her waist and began to methodically unfasten the small buttons at the back of her dress.

As her gown slipped off her shoulders, revealing her bare upper back, chills ran down her spine, and not from the coolness of the room. She shuddered, feeling exposed yet alive. Gideon's fingers danced over her neck, leaving fire in their wake. His breath was hot against her skin, the thickness of his desire in the air and pressing against her stomach.

As their lips met again, their tongues danced and explored, mapping out the familiar terrain of each other's mouths. She could taste the brandy on his lips, a reminder of the countless stolen moments they had shared. His hands roamed her bare back, his touch sending shivers down her spine.

He explored the small of her back before sliding his hands up her spine and reaching the delicate laces of her stays. She gasped, her breath hitching as he gently began unlacing the thin ribbons that held her undergarments in place.

As his fingers worked their way down her back, she erupted in gooseflesh, the heat of his hands searing her skin. His touch was tender, yet firm, sending shock through her body.

The world around them seemed to blur as they became lost in one another. The friction between their bodies as they moved together sent waves of heat coursing through her veins, igniting a fire deep within her core.

Madeline's breath became shallow and quick as his lips traced a path from her neck to her collarbone. Her heart pounded against her chest, her body trembling in anticipation as she reached her hands up and untied the cravat from around his eyes so that they could see one another when they came together.

"Gideon," she whispered, her voice barely audible above the distant sound of their friends' laughter. "I need you."

He didn't need to be told twice. He lifted her onto the sofa, her arms wrapping around his neck as he laid her down gently.

The candles flickered, casting an intimate glow over their bodies. Gideon's eyes were dark and intense, his gaze locked on her. The soft sofa beneath her body cushioned her as her legs wrapped around his hips. His hardness through his trousers pressed against her core, now bare to him but for her thin chemise, and she moaned softly into his mouth.

"Are you sure about this, Madeline?" he whispered against her lips, his low voice in such contrast to the shouts of the game outside the room. "You can change your mind."

She shook her head, her eyes locked on his. "I want this, Gideon. I need you. Now."

Her body was alight, her skin tingling with the anticipation of what was to come. She reached up and unfastened his fall for him, her fingers shaking with nerves and desire.

He allowed her to do so, the only sign of his growing impatience the tick in his cheek from where he held his jaw tightly together. Finally, he sprang free of his breeches, and Madeline swallowed hard.

For she suddenly realized just how large he was – and that he was supposed to fit inside her.

"Gideon," she said nervously, "are you sure this is going to work?"

"Very sure," he said. "I promise you that I will make certain it will go smoothly."

He kissed her again, holding her hair back away from her face as his other hand drew a path down her body, stopping at her ankle and beginning to inch up again, only this time beneath her chemise instead of above it. She shivered and he paused, leaning back from her but keeping his hand where it was before he swept a blanket over the two of them.

"Better?" he murmured, and she nodded as his hand

reached her hip, splaying across it while his thumb hit her centre, and she nearly jumped off the sofa, even as she remembered all he had done with that expert hand before.

He massaged her, relieving her of many of her worries as she relaxed into him, his thumb circling, his fingers beginning to stroke. The desire that had been so present before began to return, until she found herself rocking into his hand, desperate for more.

"Now, Gideon, please," she murmured, not wanting to feel her pleasure entirely with his hand, but along with him.

He nodded, moving slightly as his cock pressed against her entrance. He guided himself with one hand, the other sliding up to play with one of her nipples. She gasped at the sensation of the two different areas of her body, as he stroked, kneaded, and tweaked her breasts until her nipples were peaked, sending sensations down to the centre where he was slowly easing into her.

There was a brief moment of pain, highlighted by her uncertainty, but as soon as her worry began to overwhelm her, he slid out, then in again a fair distance farther. He continued to rock back and forth, entering her so slowly that she didn't notice how far he was until he was fully seated within her.

A drop of sweat laced his brow, and she reached up, whisking it away as he held still, allowing her to grow used to him.

"That's it," he said, leaning in and raining kisses over her cheeks. "Relax for me."

She took a breath, realizing how much easier it was when she did as he said. She showed him that she wanted more by arching into him, yearning for him to take her higher, and he began to rock in and out once more, this time providing her with friction as his pelvis hit hers in exactly the right place.

"Yes," she said, as he became the one in charge now, the

confident one willing to show her all that was and all that could be between the two of them. "Make me yours, Gideon."

"You already are," he said hoarsely, "and you always will be."

He continued to thrust into her, his words causing her to move even closer to the edge that was awaiting her. When he reached down and began to knead his thumb over the sensitive swell between her legs, she began to lose her sight as the world turned black, leaving her as blind as he had been with the cravat over his eyes.

"Gideon!" she cried out as she began to tremble around him, and with a cry he let go of all the reserve that had been holding him back as his movements became more rapid, more hurried, until he let out a cry that was near animalistic as he found his own release, holding her close against him as he gave her all of him.

They stayed locked together as Madeline came back to herself, blinking as she realized that the darkness had been caused by squeezing her eyes shut to the point that she had lost herself in the moment – in Gideon.

"Did that really just happen?" she whispered, and he stroked her hair, leaning back to look into her eyes, the dim light casting shadows of the two of them locked in their embrace on the wall behind him.

"Do you regret it?" he asked.

"Never," she said fiercely. "No matter what happens, that was the best thing that ever happened to me."

"Then let's do it again, as much as we'd like, for all the years that we might have," he said. "Will you marry me? Will you be my wife?"

A small, nearly imperceptible whisper at the back of her head questioned if this was enough, his offer only when he felt that he no longer needed what another woman could give, but she immediately silenced it. He was only being the responsible lord he must be. It was not as though he had ever wanted another. She had been the woman that he had yearned for, that he had shown his affection for even if he hadn't been able to offer for her.

"Of course," she said, leaning in and kissing him chastely compared to their previous kisses. "I would want nothing more."

It was at that moment a loud banging on the door had them both jumping.

"Come out, you two!" Devon called. "We found another bottle of brandy."

Gideon and Madeline stared at one another in shock for a moment, before she couldn't help it. She started to laugh and he soon followed, as they knew their friends held no judgement but would certainly not hold back from merciless jesting.

Gideon took the blanket and began to clean Madeline up with it before he cast it in the corner and then leaned down and found her stays and gown. He helped her into both, somehow his redressing and retying more intimate than the act of removing them had been.

"Well," he said, holding out a hand after he had set himself to rights, "are you ready to return?"

"With you," she said with a smile before she clasped his outstretched hand, "always."

CHAPTER 21

Gideon awoke the next morning with a smile on his face – one that he wasn't sure was ever going to leave him.

Madeline had agreed to be his wife, after what had been the most unbelievable coming together, even if it was likely ill-advised as they had yet to be wed.

It had been worth the ribbing that had accompanied their emergence from the front parlor. Of course, no one knew the full extent of what had occurred in there, but he had a sense that most of them guessed what was close to the truth.

They had agreed to keep their engagement news between themselves, at least until Gideon had a chance to speak with Madeline's father, who was due to arrive to collect his daughter in the next week. In the meantime, Gideon would have loved to have spent the night with Madeline by his side, but he didn't want to chance the repercussions of what it could mean for their families' reputations. While their servants were few and loyal, they still talked, and his mother would be beside herself if she knew that she had completely failed in her duties as a chaperone.

THE HEIR'S FORTUNE

Gideon headed upstairs that morning with the intent to share with his father the results of their treasure hunt, but his father's most loyal servant, his valet and aid, Anderson, told him that his father was not having the best of mornings.

Perhaps it would be best to wait until he had the treasure in front of him. It might make more sense to his father that way.

"Well?" Gideon said to the men that morning once they had all risen, earlier than usual. "Are we ready?"

"Of course," Ferrington said. "While the adventure has subsided, I would still like to see this treasure in your stores and all set to rights. Are we prepared for anyone that might try to intercept us?"

"We are," Gideon answered affirmatively as he placed his own pistols in their holsters. He was not the best shot – he would prefer closer combat such as fencing – but this would have to do given the circumstances.

All of the men nodded their agreement before the women joined them in the foyer.

"Are you certain this is the best idea?" Cassandra asked, crossing her arms over her chest. "Perhaps we should ask some of the local men to accompany you for greater numbers."

"I do not want to get them involved," Gideon said, shaking his head. "It is far too dangerous. At least we have all been taught how to use our weapons and are prepared for such a fight."

"Very well," Cassandra said, although Gideon's eyes were on Madeline alone. She stood in the doorway, arms crossed over her chest as she stared at him with something akin to fear in her eyes – an emotion he wasn't sure that he had ever seen upon her before. "Be safe."

The other gentlemen said their farewells to their wives, and Gideon longed to go over and wrap Madeline in his embrace, but, for now, their affection would have to remain private. Instead, he stared her way, hoping that she would understand from his expression what he felt and what he most wanted to say to her.

Gideon had two wagons brought around to the front of the house, insisting that he and Devon could drive them without the help of the coachman, who seemed slighted by their dismissal, but of course, agreed.

As wary as Gideon was while they began their return to the treasure, he couldn't help the happiness that continued to engulf him, as Madeline's aura floated around him despite her remaining at the house, reminding him of all that was good in the world. Love. He hadn't been sure that he ever would have had the chance to find it – but here it was. Here *she* was.

They had no trouble finding the opening this time. Gideon had a moment of trepidation as he entered the small cut-out in the hill, a vision catching him of the cave sitting empty, all of the treasure gone as though it had just been part of his imaginings.

But no. There were all of the chests, laid out before him.

He turned around, expecting Devon to be behind him, but the small tunnel was still empty. It wouldn't be out of character for Devon to be trying to convince one of the other men to help Gideon carry all of the treasure instead of him. Gideon began to walk to the front of the cave, calling out for his friend.

"Devon, are you coming? We only have to take these as far as the entrance before the other men can help. Are you—"

He stopped when he reached the exit and was confronted by a nightmare.

There was a very good reason why Devon hadn't joined him.

It was because he was being held at gunpoint – along

THE HEIR'S FORTUNE

with his three other friends. Their idea to have two of them on the lookout hadn't worked incredibly well.

"Lord Ashford, I presume?"

Gideon looked up to find a man walking toward him, dressed in Spanish attire. His face was adorned by a small beard and a smirk.

Gideon opened his mouth to ask who he was, but Ferrington spoke first.

"*Don* Rafael," his usually jovial friend said with a growl in his voice. "I told you never to show your face here again."

"And I told you all that this treasure belonged to me," the Spaniard said in heavily accented English before turning his attention upon Gideon. "Your great-grandmother stole it from my family and I have come to see that it is rightly returned."

"We were told that your claim to it was dubious," Ferrington said.

"By whom?"

"It doesn't matter. But suffice it to say that a very credible source told us that the treasure was not yours to begin with. Besides, that was generations ago. It is here now, on Ashford's land, so his it will be."

Don Rafael scoffed. "Do you suppose that will be the case? There are two ways we can do this. The easier path forward provides you with the chance to remain alive by the end of it all. The other, not so much."

Gideon began to slowly reach for his weapon, but *Don* Rafael realized his intention before he grasp it.

"Stop!" he said, and then a smile began to spread across his face. "Besides, even if you do not care about your own life, do you not care for the life of another? Emilio!"

There was motion at the treeline – the very one where Gideon had kissed Madeline just yesterday, and then, causing his heart to sink to his toes, one of *Don* Rafael's men walked out with the woman Gideon loved held in front of him, a pistol at her head.

"Let her go!" he ground out, but *Don* Rafael only laughed.

"You saved her once before, but we will not repeat our mistakes a second time," he said. "We have also come to learn that this woman is not your sister. It was even better, however, when we discovered that she is, in actuality, the woman you are enamored with."

Gideon gritted his teeth together as he looked around at his friends, all who appeared as helpless as he felt.

"Allow me to switch places with her," he said.

"Why would I do that?" *Don* Rafael said. "It is clear that you value her life above yours."

"That is true," he said, trying to mask his desperation. "Which is why I am asking you to let her go. You have captured us and we are in no position to take the treasure from you. Allow her to return to the house and I will remain while you do what you will with the treasure."

Don Rafael squinted his eyes at him as he considered his request and Gideon said a prayer.

Finally, rubbing his chin, *Don* Rafael shook his head. "No," he said. "If I allow her to go you might attempt some hero routine. You will never subdue us but you may cause injury to one of us, which I will not have. She will remain under Emilio's… *care* until this is all finished. You and your men are going to have quite the afternoon. For you will still do as you intended – load the treasure. Only *we* will be leaving with the wagons instead of you."

His grin caused Gideon to shiver. He looked over to Devon, who solemnly held his gaze, defeat beginning to seep into his expression. With pistols drawn upon them and one pressed against Madeline's head, they had no choice – they would have to do as the Spaniards wished. Gideon's heart sank into his stomach as his body began vibrating with rage.

"Very well," he said, tilting his head toward the cave. "Let us get to work."

Gideon could have wept as he thought of the treasure returning to the Spaniards after all these years and all of the work his ancestors had done to ensure that not just anyone would find it. He also knew what this was likely going to mean for him.

It was the loss of his pride, for one – the Spaniard had outsmarted him. He hated to admit that Cassandra had been right and they would have been better to bring more men with them.

Now he was losing not only the treasure but could also lose the chance to have Madeline.

For what kind of man was he that he had lost the fortune that was supposed to allow them to have a future together? He had nothing to offer her anymore. Not only that, but he had allowed her to be captured again and had failed to protect her when she was the one person he should be doing everything to safeguard.

He was so ashamed that he couldn't even look at her. He didn't want to see the disappointment he knew would be in her eyes. It had taken her years to see him as a man worthy of her love, her trust, and in this one failure he was losing it all.

Gideon was hoping for the opportunity to speak to Devon alone once they entered the cave, as it might be their only chance to devise a potential plan to find their way out of this, but one of *Don* Rafael's men followed them in. Gideon wasn't sure how much English he could understand, but he had no desire to risk it.

Devon, of course, had no problems doing so.

"How are we getting out of this?" he hissed to Gideon as they reached down to lift the first trunk.

"I cannot see a way out of it," Gideon muttered. "We are done for. All that matters is that Madeline comes to no harm and she escapes from them. If anything happens, make sure she is safe."

Devon's head quickly swiveled toward Gideon. "What is that supposed to mean?"

"Exactly what I said," he responded before their guard began charging toward them in a flurry of Spanish, telling them to stop talking. Gideon looked at Devon with an "I told you so," before they lowered the trunk down to Whitehall and Ferrington. Rowley was waiting to help load it into the carriage.

When the trunks were finished, Gideon and Devon climbed down from the hole. Devon looked ready to charge the Spaniards, but Gideon shook his head at him, hoping he would understand. Cassandra would never forgive him if something happened to her husband.

"You have what you want. Now let her go," he called out to *Don* Rafael as he began walking toward them.

"I have to make sure we get away from here safely," *Don* Rafael said. "While you were collecting my treasure, I realized there was only one way to ensure that would be so."

"Which is?" Gideon asked with growing trepidation.

Don Rafael grinned once more. "To take the woman with us."

CHAPTER 22

This could not be happening again.

Madeline would never forgive herself for letting down her guard and allowing herself to be captured – a second time. How embarrassing. Here they had thought they were making the smart decision in staying at the house, in not providing the men something else to worry about while they retrieved the treasure.

The women had decided to pass the time in a book discussion, and Madeline had been walking alone to return to her bedroom for her book. As she had passed the front entrance, she had been taken off guard by two men who had dragged her out of the front door with a hand over her mouth and her arms behind her back.

She could only pray that her friends remained safe inside Castleton.

She now sensed Gideon's growing dejection as hope began to slip away from them, and she wished that he would fight for his treasure, fight for what he believed in, and not allow the Spaniards to get away with this.

His request to change places with her had been noble, but

she had known that the ask was futile before the Spaniards had even responded.

She had just never considered that there might be an additional threat beyond their theft of the treasure.

"I most certainly will not go with you," she said, holding her spine straight as she turned around and stared straight at *Don* Rafael, facing the pistol that he held to her head. She hoped that she maintained a façade of confidence, for inside she was shaking at the thought of what might happen next.

"And just how do you think you are going to prevent that from happening?" he asked smugly. "I do not believe your *amante* over there is going to be able to stop me."

Madeline swallowed hard, for the truth was, he was right. She had no idea just what she was going to do and Gideon would never try anything perilous when her life was at risk.

That was when the first arrow flew.

It fell in a perfect arc through the sky, landing with a thud in the middle of Emilio's chest. He had been holding his pistol behind Madeline, and she jumped as he went backward, a loud thump resounding when he hit the ground behind him.

"You must be joking!" *Don* Rafael cursed, for this was not the first time he had faced the wrath of such arrows.

For Madeline knew exactly where they came from – Faith's bowstring. And Faith was not a woman who ever missed her mark.

It was Madeline's turn to grin, and then before she even realized what was happening, they were surrounded – only this time it was *Don* Rafael's men who were surrounded, pistols trained upon them by four new men who stood around them with their faces covered. It took the gentlemen a moment to realize what was happening, but when they did, they quickly drew their weapons, as they now outnumbered the Spaniards by two to one.

"It's over, *Don* Rafael," Gideon said, his voice not triumphant but rather relieved. "You must give it up. This time, I will make sure that you will never be released."

Don Rafael's eyes frantically flicked from one side to the other, and as much as Madeline was celebrating the fact that they were now going to end this victorious, she knew that madness could make a man unpredictable. And mad *Don* Rafael was. This had been his quest for so long, and now it was all being taken away from him, with no alternate ending in sight.

He pulled the cock on the pistol all the way back and turned it toward her once more, pressing it hard against her temple.

"We might all not be saved, but the girl and I will be going now. Into the wagon," he said, pushing Madeline with his other hand. She took a breath, searching for an opportunity to escape, but she couldn't risk moving away with the gun so close to her temple. When she saw the wagon with its attached horses, she had an idea, however, one that would take some quick thinking and perfect timing, but one that just might work.

Don Rafael kept the pistol upon her while urging her to climb up onto the seat of the wagon, and as he followed after her, he still kept it up close to her as she could see the gentlemen all watching helplessly. When it was time to direct the horses, however, he realized his dilemma – he did not have enough hands.

"Drive," he ordered her, pointing to the reins.

Madeline nodded, but when she reached down to pick them up, his pistol, fortunately, remained high, near where her head had been, and she used the opportunity to throw herself off the seat and onto the horse in front of her.

She landed with a groan as the horse was not saddled and

its harnesses caused her all kinds of pain, but the horse held steady even at the sudden surprise of her weight.

It was a stout Clydesdale, not a breed she was used to riding, but one that she would be forever grateful for.

As she jumped, *Don* Rafael shouted after her, but when the pistol shot rang out, his shout turned into a cry of pain. Madeline's heart jumped when she heard him hit the wooden seat behind her, and she couldn't help her relief that he was down, as awful as that was.

Gideon was at her side in moments, but she didn't wait for him to help her down, instead sliding gracefully off the horse herself until she was standing next to it. The moment her feet hit the ground, however, his arms were around her and he was holding her close against him – so close that she had to push away ever so slightly.

"I am so sorry but I cannot breathe," she managed, although she lifted her hands to touch her palms to his cheeks. "I am so glad you are all right."

"Me?" he repeated, swiping his hand over his brow. "I am fine besides the fact that I do not think *I* breathed for the last few minutes when he held the pistol to your head. One wrong move and it all could have been over. I am so sorry, Madeline."

"Why would you be sorry?" she asked, furrowing her brow.

"Because this was all my fault," he said, shaking his head. "I never should have drawn you – or anyone else – into this."

"That we can discuss later," she said, stepping back and looking around them. "In the meantime, perhaps we should determine just who *everyone* else is."

"Quite right," he murmured, turning around, although he kept one hand firmly pressed against her lower back. "Our mysterious saviours have not fled as they have in the past."

As they left the horses and wagons and walked toward the

men who were currently occupied with containing the Spaniards, Gideon leaned down and whispered in her ear. "Behind me, just in case."

"Gideon—"

"Please," he said, with so much supplication that she couldn't help but agree, noting that their friends were gathered on one side of the clearing, the gentlemen standing in front to protect the women, although Madeline guessed that Faith was likely just as competent to keep them safe with her bow and arrow.

The Spaniards were now tied up and sitting in one of the wagons that was currently empty, while the gentlemen were on the other side, warily watching the men who had appeared in their hour of need.

"There's nothing to fear, Gideon," Cassandra called out, and Madeline realized then that the women had been working with these men, likely after she had been taken, although how it had all come about was a mystery that she was looking forward to learning more about.

One of their heroes lifted his head, his face, rather weathered and yet fairly strong, becoming clear from beneath his hat.

He looked familiar, but Madeline couldn't immediately place him. It seemed Gideon, however, could.

His mouth dropped as he gaped at the man. "Anderson?"

* * *

GIDEON COULDN'T HELP but take a step back in surprise at seeing his father's valet and attendant staring back at him, nearly knocking over Madeline as he did so for he forgot that she was standing right behind him.

"But how—"

"It's a long story," Anderson said, walking over to him and

lifting a hand as though he was about to place it on his shoulder before dropping it, likely remembering their difference in station, even though Anderson had known him since he was a child. "Perhaps one we best tell away from here, once we can be more comfortable. We accompanied the women here once we heard that Madeline had gone missing again. They trusted us but are waiting for an explanation as well."

Gideon nodded slowly as he looked around at the rest of them. There was Victor, the stablehand; Jacobs, the butler; and John, one of the footmen. Even their old groundskeeper, the one he'd had to let go because he could no longer afford for him to take care of the grounds, was with them.

"One question before we go," Gideon said, needing to know. "Did you come today because Cassandra asked for your help to find Madeline, or has it been you helping us the entire time?"

"We've been with you every step of the way," Anderson said. "For far longer than you might guess."

Gideon was trying to piece it all together, frustrated with himself for not seeing this sooner when Cassandra stepped forward. "Why do we not meet in the billiards room?"

"The billiards room?" he repeated. It was not a place for ladies and he had the feeling that these women were not going to miss this conversation.

"It has room for us all," she said before stepping near him and murmuring, "and they will likely feel more comfortable there as it is closer to the servants' quarters and Mother isn't likely to come upon us."

"Very well," he said, immediately understanding and appreciating Cassandra's sense when it came to such matters. She was right, of course. They couldn't exactly bring the men in to sit in his mother's drawing room without a good explanation, now could they?

"First, we must send for the magistrate," Gideon said, pointing to the remaining Spaniards. They hadn't even checked to see if *Don* Rafael was alive. Madeline began to point that out to Gideon, but the footman was already walking over to do so.

"One of us will go for him," Victor said. "Take the women back to Castleton and we could meet in an hour, if that is sufficient for you?"

"Very well," Gideon said, nodding his thanks to the stablehand. They had waited this long. What was a few more minutes? He looked to the other men, finding Devon standing on the other side of Cassandra. "Let's get these wagons back to the stables and see the women inside. I'll walk back with them."

Madeline looked up at him, her eyes wide. "You are not going to ride with the treasure?"

"No," he said. "I rather think that I have the treasure right here beside me."

"How romantic," she said, leaning back and away from him with a smile. "And how fortunate that we were to get the actual treasure back, is it not?"

There was a bite within her tone, one that he couldn't quite understand, but he didn't comment upon it, not now when they had finally set everything to rights. He had the fortune he had been chasing, he had Madeline, *Don* Rafael appeared to be dead, and it seemed that he was going to receive some answers.

He truly couldn't ask for anything more.

CHAPTER 23

As it turned out, it was a bit more than an hour by the time they had all gathered in the billiards room. It had taken time to store the treasure, ensure that it was under proper lock and key, see to the horses, and become presentable enough that they would be able to make the dinner hour after their meeting with the servants in the billiard's room.

Madeline still wasn't quite meeting Gideon's eye, which he didn't like – not at all. But that was another mystery he supposed he would have to solve later. He had enough concerns at the moment.

She still sat next to him, although they were not particularly close to one another as they had each taken one of the chairs that lined the wall, usually reserved for other gentlemen, Scout sitting at attention between them. He had remained at home when they went for the treasure and now was sitting so attentively, as though he had to ensure that he wasn't left behind again. The servants sat across from them, and it seemed that Anderson was going to take the lead and speak for them.

"What would you like to know?" Anderson asked, appearing the most comfortable of them all, as he had spent most of his life in the house, living next to Gideon's father and accompanying him in most of his daily activities.

"Everything," Gideon said, but before Anderson could start, Scout's head turned, his ear twitching up as another presence filled the doorway.

"Mother?" Gideon exclaimed as she stopped abruptly, looking around at the lot of them with a shocked expression. "What are you doing here?"

"I was looking for Anderson," she said. "Your father is particularly lucid and he would like to go riding. What is happening?"

Gideon saw his father hovering behind her, and, after a moment of hesitation in which he wondered if he was making the right decision, he waved them in. They deserved this story as much as anyone else, especially now that there was no danger remaining for his mother to worry about. "Come in. You might as well learn all of this at the same time."

"All of what?"

"It has to do with the treasure that I had asked you both about."

"Very well," she said, walking in with his father, who looked to Anderson instead of Gideon.

"Anderson? What is happening?"

"I will explain all," he said while John and the groundskeeper appeared even more uncomfortable in a room full of lords, ladies, and now a duke and duchess.

Anderson took a breath before he began his story.

"As you know, my father worked here until his retirement and raised me in this house. He was the one who told me that working here at Castleton meant more than just regular servant duties. It came with an element of protection if you will."

"Protection?" Gideon repeated. "What do we need protection from?"

Anderson chuckled lowly. "From the very people we saved you from."

Gideon nodded, feeling foolish as Anderson continued.

"It was not just you who needed protection, however. We were sent to protect the treasure as well."

Gideon's jaw tightened at the news that servants within his very household had known not only about the treasure but where it was located, while he had raced around like a fool searching for it.

"You knew about the treasure this entire time?" Gideon said, trying to control his ire.

"We have known since we were told about it by those who came before us," Anderson said. "When your great-grandmother and great-grandfather brought the treasure here from Spain seventy years ago, they were accompanied by men loyal to them. They hid the treasure and knew they needed someone they could trust to look over it. They chose loyal servants, who vowed to always watch out for the treasure until the timing was right for someone worthy to find it."

"I don't understand."

"You will," Anderson said. "My father worked here, as did his father. The legacy was passed down to me." He waved to the rest of the servants. "As it was for them."

"Did you know we were searching for it?"

"We were not aware at first," Anderson said, exchanging a look with the groundskeeper. "There were a couple of accidents that were entirely our fault as we thought someone else was after it and we were trying to scare them away."

"The shot in the woods?" Devon asked. "When Cassandra

and I were searching for the cabins?"

"That was one of us, yes," Anderson admitted. "We didn't realize it was the two of you. Our sincerest apologies."

"What about Anthony's accident?" Hope demanded in an uncharacteristically demanding tone. "He nearly died when his horse was startled."

"That wasn't us," Anderson said. "*Don* Rafael had sent a man to scout the area and see if he could determine where the treasure might be. He was coming after you and tried to shoot. We were, however, able to stop him from doing any more damage."

"Thank you," Whitehall said, and Hope reached over and grasped his hand, likely realizing just how much worse it could have been.

"Do you know who stole the necklace from Cassandra's Aunt Eve in Bath?" Percy interjected.

"Mrs. Compton's lady's maid is aware of the treasure and the legacy, and we were able to exchange letters with her. It seems that the necklace truly was stolen the first time by another maid, who pawned it off, which is how it fell into the hands of another. The second time it was stolen, it was her lady's maid, who decided the best course of action would be to take the necklace herself and return it to Castleton so that it didn't fall into the wrong hands again."

Percy nodded with some wonder.

"When Lady Faith and Lord Ferrington left for Spain, we wrote to Abello to tell him who they were. He has been part of this along with us since he knew your great-grandmother, Lord Ashford. He responded to our letter, telling us that he suspected *Don* Rafael was aware of your true identities. We knew to be prepared when you returned."

"Unbelievable," the duke said, and they all turned to him, uncertain of just how he would react to this. "Did my father have any idea?"

"No," Anderson said. "We were asked to keep this to ourselves until the timing was right and the treasure was found."

"The real question is, why did they hide it?" Gideon asked, sitting forward. "When they returned to England, why not use the treasure, put it back into the dukedom?"

Although, he was pleased that they didn't, for it would have all been squandered away as well.

"Because it wasn't the proper time to return the treasure to where it belonged."

Gideon didn't like that response.

"Which is... where?"

"Upper Peru," Anderson said, a smile lighting his face. "My grandfather was from the country and, in fact, sailed with your great-grandparents along with the treasure from Spain to England. The Spanish mined the mountains of Upper Peru for the metals that forged the doubloons. *Don* Rafael's great-grandfather, who was your great-grandmother Mariana's first husband, stole it from the government with the help of pirates. When your great-grandparents found it, at first they weren't sure just who it belonged to, but they realized where it was from and to where it should return."

Gideon was beginning to understand just what Anderson was saying, and as noble as the intentions had been, he was fighting the reality of what it was going to mean for him and the people who relied on him.

"It is no different than what we have done here in Britain for years. When countries are part of our colony, they utilize their resources accordingly. Spain did the same."

"Perhaps," Anderson said, sitting back, crossing his arms over his chest. "But if France were to defeat Britain, would you think Napoleon deserves all that England has to offer?"

Gideon took a breath and a moment to consider just what Anderson was saying before the man continued.

"Your great-grandparents had the noble purpose of returning the treasure to where it belonged – Upper Peru. The Spanish have mined it for centuries, using the labour of my ancestors and my people today to bring it to the surface. Spanish rule now is tenuous at best. It will not be long before my people find their independence once more, I am sure of it. This treasure, in the right hands, could help them in their quest. Your great-grandparents could not return it at the time because Spanish rule was too strong. They were hoping a time would come in the future when it could be returned to its proper place."

"Which is now?"

"If you do what they were hoping, then yes," Anderson said. "Do you have any more questions?"

Gideon looked to his father, who was stroking his chin in contemplation but said nothing.

"I do not believe we do at the moment, but perhaps once we consider it further. This is rather overwhelming." In fact, Gideon felt as though he had been lied to for years, that all along, the people he had trusted, who had looked after Castleton, had known what was hiding just a short distance away and had said nothing, leaving him to look the fool.

"I am aware of that," Anderson said. "I know the treasure is found but I still consider myself to be at your service with whatever you might need of me. I still have family connections back home that I can use to return the treasure and to ensure it will go to those who deserve it most."

Gideon began nodding, even as he realized exactly what this meant. The treasure – the one that he had thought meant he had restored the dukedom to rights, that he no longer had to worry about marrying for a dowry because the fortune had refilled the coffers – was gone. It was not his, nor had it ever been.

Which meant that all had returned to exactly how it had

been before. A dukedom in ruin, a crumbling estate, people who depended on him disappointed, and few paths forward.

Not only that, but he had lost all of that time he had spent hunting for the treasure, time that he could have been using in more worthwhile pursuits.

He had thought that he had everything he needed to offer for Madeline.

But it was as it had been before.

He was insolvent and alone.

* * *

MADELINE HAD REMAINED silent as she had listened to the servant's story. Everyone in the room had sat in rapt attention as he had explained the mysteries that had surrounded them while also telling them of the path forward.

She knew, with a growing sense of dread deep in her stomach, what this meant.

It was not that she was concerned that the fortune wasn't Gideon's. It was how he would react, what he would think that he had to do instead.

Say goodbye to her.

She couldn't hear it. Madeline didn't want those words, the words that would tell her she would come second, and only when all had worked out. She wanted to be his first choice, wanted to be worth more than anything else. She wanted to know that they could find a way forward together.

But that wasn't Gideon. He was a man of responsibility, of doing the right thing and taking care of others, even to the detriment of himself.

So instead of hearing the words of goodbye, perhaps it would be best for her to say them first, before he could hurt her and tell her that a fortune was more important than she was, that he was going to take the easy way out and marry for money instead, choosing it over what they shared, that she had thought was going to mean forever.

She wasn't upset that she had given her body to him. She loved him, and that had been worth it, whether or not they would remain together.

It was that he might throw it all away over something so trivial.

Perhaps it would be for the best. All along, as right as it had felt to be together, there was something wrong in it as well. It was almost as though she was the prize for him to have achieved what he had set out for and not the partner who could do it with him.

"It has been a long day," the duchess said, standing, her smile serene despite all they had just discovered and gone through. "Why do we all not rest for a time, and then have dinner? We shall make sure that all of you eat well tonight." She paused. "Well, we will do our best."

There were some grimaces at the thought of dinner and Gideon must have come to the realization as well.

"Our cook…"

"She is part of it, yes," Anderson said. "She feels great loyalty to the family."

"Which is why we have kept her with us, yes," Gideon said, running a hand through his hair. "I never understood why she stayed when we did not pay her as a cook deserves."

"Perhaps she can find another position in our house soon that she would be better suited for," the duchess said. "A lady's maid, perhaps?"

She said it with such a hopeful smile that Madeline knew exactly what she was thinking – perhaps a lady's maid for a new addition to their home. The only question was whether it would be her, or someone else entirely.

CHAPTER 24

"This is all rather unbelievable, is it not?" Cassandra said to Gideon.

They were seated on the floor of the long gallery where the chests had been stored and the treasure laid out before them. They had decided to review and inventory it all before they determined how to go about returning it to its proper home.

"It is," he murmured. "All of it is unbelievable. That we were sent on this treasure hunt, that we found chests full of literal treasure, and now, after everything we went through, we are only going to be returning it."

"I sense a bitterness in there," Cassandra said, stopping her count of the coins to look at him after writing down the number so she wouldn't forget it. "I know you were hoping that this treasure would restore our family fortunes, but it is not as though something was stolen from us. This was never ours to begin with."

"I suppose you're right," he said, his jaw tight. "I just..." he sighed. He hadn't planned on talking to his sister about this, but she knew Madeline better than anyone, knew him and understood this situation. Perhaps she could provide some insight into his dilemma – one that was eating at him. He knew that Madeline was waiting for him to speak to her, but the truth was, he had no idea just what he was supposed to say to her. "I just thought that if the treasure allowed us to recompense all that we had lost, I would not have to resort to doing so by any other means."

"I do hope you are not referring to the idea of marrying a woman for her dowry," Cassandra said with a frown of disdain.

"And what if I am?" he asked defensively. "I would hardly be the first to do so. In fact, it would be more common than not."

"But most of the men who do so are not in love with another woman!" she exclaimed. "Especially a woman who loves him back."

"She said that?" He couldn't help but hold onto those words, and Cassandra shook her head at him before looking away and up at one of the sculptures that lined the room, this one of a man who appeared quite handsome, wrapped in a toga and looking to the sky in supplication.

One of their ancestors had been greatly interested in the Greeks and had amassed the statues that stood before them now. Gideon wondered if it was time to begin selling them, even if it was telling all that their family was giving up.

"She has said almost nothing to me," Cassandra said, her eyes glinting. "However, the two of you do nothing but stare at one another longingly every time you are together, and when you each speak of the future, I get the sense that you are picturing a future *together*."

"I thought I was free, Cassandra," he said, hearing the anguish in his voice, hating himself for it but, for one of the first times in his life, allowing himself to feel and voice the emotion that was inside of him. "Free to marry the woman I chose. Free of the burden of letting down all of the people who rely on us. Free to be enough, as myself, for the first time in my life."

"And now you believe all that has changed because you no longer have the treasure?"

"I believe that I should see to all the people that I am responsible for. But I did offer for Madeline, and I am a man of my word. I cannot take that request back."

"Trust me, Gideon, the last thing that Madeline would want is for you to marry her against your will. If you still want to marry her, it has to be because that is what you truly want and not what you feel obligated to do."

He paused, allowing her words to sink in, and she continued before he could respond.

"Since you were rid of all of the stewards and men of business who caused our financial ruin, what has happened?"

"I have done all I can to rebuild."

"Doing everything yourself."

"I cannot trust anyone else."

"And?" She raised a brow.

"And I have begun to restore some of the money we lost."

"*We* didn't lose it. Others lost it for us."

"It was still under our watch."

She nodded in agreement.

"I cannot say that I know much about running an estate," she said. "But if you were to invest in everything needed to be successful, could you take us down that road that much quicker? I know you are conservative and safe, but sometimes you have to take a chance. What if you hired back some of the people you needed to work the land, the gardens? What if you made some investments that just might be worth something? You could take us far, Gideon, because you know what? This dukedom is not a sum of its parts. It is not Castleton, it is not what is in its coffers, it is not what it produces.

It is who is part of it. Who *we* are. It's the people who surround us. You can make the dukedom whatever it is you want it to be. And let me ask you something – who do you think is going to help you do that? A nameless woman who has been bred to do as she has been told to do, who will know that she means nothing to you but what her dowry can provide, or a woman who loves you, who is willing to take those risks that you don't, who can be your other half in every sense of the word?"

Gideon stilled, hopeful, inspired, and yet… afraid.

He was afraid to believe his sister, afraid that she was right. For if she was, that meant that he had to leap forward in a direction that scared him.

"What if I do marry Madeline but then I continue to lose everything?" he asked. "What kind of life is that for her?"

Cassandra looked at him with a brow raised in skepticism.

"First, the chance of that happening is low, for I know you, Gideon, and you would not allow that to happen," she said. "Secondly, that is her choice to make. You have kept nothing secret from her. She knows what awaits her, and she can decide if it is worth taking the chance. If *you* are worth taking the chance."

"What if she says no?" he said grimly, not wanting to think about that option, of putting himself out there, without the treasure, with a dukedom that was still falling to ruin.

"Then she says no," Cassandra said simply, "and you move on with that loss. But then at least you have tried."

"Then at least I've tried," he muttered. "Very well."

"The fact that you are even sharing this with me and asking for my opinion says a lot," Cassandra said. "There were times you would barely speak to me at all, let alone ask what I thought."

"Cassandra, I—"

"I know. It wasn't just me. You were like that with everyone. Except Devon, perhaps."

Gideon nodded his agreement.

"You are a good man, Gideon," she said softly. "You always do what is right, and you do so much for everyone else. Sometimes, however, you have to do something for yourself to be better for all of those around you."

Gideon reflected on the last few years, of how empty he had been. How, with Madeline in his life, he had found a sense of purpose, and not just in finding the treasure, but in his life itself.

"You're right," he said with a sense of wonder.

"Of course I am right," she said with a slight snort.

He stood, beginning to walk to the door.

"Where are you going?" she asked, raising her hands at all that surrounded her. He knew they still had much left to accomplish, but if he didn't go now, he might never go.

"I have to talk to Madeline."

"Now?" his sister said, her mouth open. "But we've only just begun!"

"I know," he said, "and I'm sorry. I will return to help you, I promise. But if I do not go speak to her now—"

"Then you might lose all of this courage that I have instilled in you?"

He couldn't help but chuckle. "Yes. Exactly."

"Very well," she said. "Go. Make my friend – and yourself – happy. You will find a way forward, Gideon. I am sure of it."

He nodded as he opened the door, stopping when she called out to him again.

"Oh, and Gideon?"

"Yes?"

"If you see Devon, please ask him to join me. I could use

some help. He started this with me. He might as well help me to finish it."

"Of course," he said, continuing down the corridor, past the paintings of his ancestors who lined the wall.

He stopped in front of the painting of his great-grandmother and great-grandfather. Their portrait had always been his favorite, but he had never been certain why. Now, as he stared at it, he better understood. They were not posed, nor sitting. They were standing, but instead of facing the painter, they were side by side, his arm around her back. They were turned partway toward one another, her mouth curled up in a half-smile, his in a full-on grin. The love between them was evident, even through the canvas and brush of the painter.

It hit him then. This treasure had been an adventure, yes, but perhaps the fortune wasn't in what was found in the chests in the cave. Perhaps it was something else entirely.

Instead of walking in trepidation now, he hurried down the stairs with renewed purpose. He had to see Madeline – and he had to see her now.

* * *

MADELINE WAS SITTING on the floor of the drawing room on a blanket, little Jack on one side of her, and Scout on the other. The dog was overly gentle with the baby – it was Jack who was the one to watch out for, as he didn't seem to know his own strength. Fortunately, Scout had a great amount of patience, simply moving out of the way whenever the baby attempted to grab a fistful of fur.

Madeline couldn't help but laugh despite the ball of melancholy that had lodged itself in her chest, threatening to explode within her.

"Lady Madeline?"

She looked up to find the butler standing in the doorway somewhat hesitantly.

"Yes, Jacobs?"

"You have a visitor."

Her heart began beating even harder as she waited for Gideon to appear, but it wasn't Gideon. Another familiar figure filled the doorway. One with hair as dark as her own, a beard that was only beginning to turn salt and pepper, and a handsome, if weathered, face.

"Father?"

"Madeline, you look well," he said as he entered, striding over and taking a seat on the sofa beside her. He had always treated her the same, even when she was a child – as though she was an acquaintance, someone to converse with instead of look after.

"Thank you," she said. "This is Jack, Cassandra's son."

He nodded, not particularly interested in the child – but then, he never had been, had he?

"Fine-looking child," he said, his foot bobbing up and down. "We do not need pleasantries, though, Madeline, do we?"

"We do not."

They never had.

"I will get right to it, then. I do not have long until I have to return to London."

"For…"

"There's a tournament."

There was always a tournament. Her father was a gambler, but unlike most, he played games of skill – poker, usually – and most often he won. She had asked him to teach her how to win as he did, but despite his less-than-upright pastimes, he had always insisted that she remain respectable. It was the one way he had always chosen to honor her mother, who would have wished it to be so.

"What does that have to do with me?" she asked.

"I was to come collect you this week upon my return to London. So here I am. I also decided it was time I find a wife and I supposed you could help me pick one. But we must leave today."

Her jaw dropped. "First, finding a wife is more than just *picking* one. And I can hardly leave today. I am not at all prepared and I would prefer more time to say my farewells to Cassandra."

He sighed. "I thought you might say that. Tomorrow then."

She narrowed her eyes. He had obviously always been planning on tomorrow. He was negotiating, as always. One would think she would have learned by now.

If this was yesterday, she would have told him no, that she would not be accompanying him to London because she was staying at Castleton indefinitely.

Now, she had no idea what to expect. The fact that Gideon had not even sought her out to speak to her, however, told her more than she would like.

"What am I to do while you are playing poker and courting women in London?"

"The Season starts soon," he said, the hope in his eyes slight, having dimmed considerably over the years as each Season passed without any success in marrying her off. "Perhaps this is your year. You could have one of these of your own!" He waved a finger around at Jack.

She looked up at him and smiled sarcastically. "You would like that, wouldn't you?"

She knew that he just wanted to be rid of her. He had done his duty by her and now was ready to live a life without being responsible for her. How different he was from Gideon, who took on responsibility with such determination to do right by those who relied on him.

Which made her realize that he would insist on keeping his promise of marriage due to having provided his word, even if he would resent it in the future. She wouldn't have that.

She had known the moment the promise of the treasure had been taken away from him that he had seen the error of his ways. She just hadn't wanted to acknowledge it.

"Very well," she said with a sigh. "I will accompany you. I will be ready by tomorrow."

"Wonderful," he said, slapping his hands on his thighs. "I'm going for a ride if you would like to join me?"

It was the one interest they had always shared, the one that had allowed them to bond when it had never been possible in any other way.

She waved toward Jack. "I cannot just leave the baby."

"There's a nanny around here somewhere, isn't there? Why are you tending to him anyway?"

She rolled her eyes. "I will see you," she said, turning her attention back to Jack, partly to hide the tears that pricked her eyes at the thought of leaving Jack, Cassandra, and now, Gideon most of all.

CHAPTER 25

"Jacobs?" Gideon called out as his search for Madeline had, thus far, proved fruitless. "Have you seen Lady Madeline?"

"She is in the drawing room," the butler said. "She is there with a visitor. Her father, Lord Trenton, has arrived."

Her father? Perfect. He would be able to ask the man for her hand in marriage – assuming Madeline agreed. Perhaps they would be able to finish all this before the man even left.

He heard the voices coming from within the drawing room and he stopped outside the door, waiting for them to finish their conversation. He would ask to speak to Madeline alone first.

He could only hope that she would still choose him.

"Very well," he heard Madeline say. "I will accompany you. I will be ready by tomorrow."

Accompany him? Where was she going?

Before he could reconsider his actions, he knocked on the door and pushed it open.

"Lord Ashford," Madeline's father, Lord Trenton, said as

he got to his feet. "Thank you for allowing my daughter to stay at your home for so long."

Gideon had never known him well, although he was aware of his reputation as a gambler – one of the reasons Madeline had told him she would only add more scandal to his name. Gideon had seen for a moment, however, what it would be like if Madeline was no longer in his life when the pistol had been held to her head. It was not a life that he had any wish to partake in. Any scandal from her father would be forgotten and forgiven when she was a future duchess.

"The pleasure is ours," Gideon said, clasping his hands behind his back and nodding his head. "Where are you going from here?"

"We will be returning to London," Lord Trenton said. "I have... business, and Madeline will continue her search for a husband."

"Will she now?" Gideon said, lifting a brow as he sought out Madeline's gaze, but she refused to meet his stare, instead suddenly very interested in what Jack was doing on the blanket beside her. "Do you have any prospective matches, Lady Madeline?"

Her eyes finally lifted to meet his.

"It can be difficult due to my lack of dowry."

Lord Trenton gave a huff as he tried to brush off her words. "Oh, come now, Maddy, it isn't that bad. I might not be able to pay someone to take you off of my hands, but I am sure one of these days a gentleman will see what a catch you are – what you can bring to a marriage."

"I am sure he will," Gideon murmured. "He will be a lucky man, indeed, if you were to ever choose him."

Madeline pleaded with him with her eyes, but Gideon was done with this game. He needed to speak to her, needed her to understand what had changed and what he intended.

"When you have finished your conversation, there is

something I would like to speak to you about, Madeline," he said as she pushed tendrils of her hair back behind her ears. "Would you join me in the gardens?"

"Of course," she said, smiling at him, although her smile didn't quite reach her eyes, disconcerting him.

He nodded and backed out the door. He didn't like how she reacted to him, didn't appreciate the idea that she hadn't said anything about him to her father, who seemed to think that she was going to be accompanying him to London. The fact that she intended to look for a husband was nearly laughable.

It was time she understood how important she was and what she meant to him.

And then he was never letting her go again.

* * *

MADELINE HAD TRIED to devise an excuse as to why she couldn't speak to Gideon, but then she reminded herself that she was not a coward but rather a woman who faced everything in her life head-on.

And so, she found herself waiting by the fountain an hour later, gently throwing pebbles into the water.

Gideon hadn't specified where in the gardens he would like to meet, but most of it was rather overgrown, although Madeline could see the beauty it held within, and she had to actively prevent herself from beginning to imagine just what she would do with it if she were to become part of the Sutcliffe family – because that just wouldn't likely be the case anymore.

She heard his steps crunching through the gravel on the path behind her before she saw him, and when she turned her head toward him, she tried not to allow him to affect her as much as he had in the past.

But it was nearly impossible. She hated how fast her heart started beating, her pulse resounding in her head. He was everything she could have ever wanted in a man, that she had never known she had needed.

And for a moment, he had been hers.

"The gardens might have been a bad idea," he said as he approached, his cloak billowing in the wind. "I had thought we would be able to spend time alone, but there is quite the chill in the air."

"Winter is coming," she said. "Soon enough it will be the Christmas season."

He held out a hand to her and she took it as she rose to meet him.

"I have an idea of what I would like that season to look like," he said, a small, wistful smile on his face as he looked off into the distance.

"Do you now?" she said, tilting her head, wondering if he meant it or if it had all just been a dream. She could see it as well. The two of them settled into the house, a hearty fire roaring behind them while greenery surrounded the room. Perhaps she would even capture him under the mistletoe. And she knew exactly what she would gift him. "Will Cassandra be staying at Castleton?"

He smiled sadly and shook his head ruefully. "I think not. She has her own family now, and they have been at Castleton longer than expected. I shouldn't be greedy in wanting anymore of their time."

"At least you have your parents with you," she said, keeping her hands to herself even when he offered her his arm to walk beside him. It hurt too much to touch him.

"Madeline," he said, stopping when they were behind a hedgerow, keeping them hidden from both the house and the wind. He placed his hands gently on her elbows, holding her there in front of him, his touch light enough that she could move away if she chose to do so. "Why are you acting as though we mean nothing to one another? That we are not promised to each other?"

She took a breath, telling herself to be stoic, to be strong, not to show him how devastated she was going to be when the time came to part.

"You have to return the treasure," she said, unable to hold his gaze for a moment, having to turn her head to look off toward the tree line in the far distance where they had raced when she had first arrived, when she had begun to see him as more than Cassandra's brother. "That means that you are once again in the same position. Of needing to marry for a dowry. A dowry that I most certainly do not have."

She tried to smile but her lip trembled instead, and she had to bite down on it to prevent him from noticing.

It appeared, however, that she had failed.

"Madeline," he said, shaking his head, the smallest of smiles gracing his face. She was so enraptured with how handsome he was that a tear fell from her eye. It took her so by surprise that she didn't have a chance to wipe it away before he reached out and did so for her. "There is no reason to cry."

As it was too late to hide her feelings from him, she let the tears flow, unable to prevent them from falling anymore.

"Of course there is reason!" she exclaimed, reaching up her hand and swatting him on the arm with it. "I do not know what I truly mean to you, but you—you mean *everything* to me."

He stilled, his eyes darkening.

"Truly?"

"How could you not know that?"

"I knew I meant something to you," he said, his blue eyes glinting at her as they widened. "But... everything?"

Embarrassed now, Madeline began backing away from

him. She hadn't meant to tell him how she felt. She had agreed to meet with him with the sole purpose of telling him that she was done with him before he had a chance to do it first, but instead, here she was, baring her soul.

"Madeline," he said softly. "Where are you going? I have never heard anything better."

"You... what?" she repeated, blinking at him. He was not the type of man to make light of such feelings, but why would he say such a thing?

"You said that nothing has changed, that everything is back to as it was before."

"It is true, is it not?" she said stubbornly.

"No," he said, shaking his head. "Not even close. Before I knew you, yes, but I wasn't *aware* of you and all of who you are. I hadn't seen what life could be like having been with you. Then when there was the possibility of you being taken away from me, I realized that life wouldn't be worth living without you. Before, I wasn't in love with you."

She heard the swift intake of her breath before she even realized what she was doing, and then found herself blinking rapidly up at him.

"You... you love me?"

"With everything that I am," he said, the corners of his lips widening into a smile. "I think I loved you from the first moment that you allowed Scout to lick you across the face and you didn't back away in disgust. For all these years, I have known you and yet never saw the woman you truly were, and how perfect that you were for me."

She already began shaking her head, blinking away the tears that threatened her again. "That was my fault. I kept you at a distance, after Cassandra—"

He cupped her face with his warm, strong hands, brushing away her tears once more with the pads of his thumbs. "You have every right to feel as you choose to feel, and I did do something to Cassandra that was so insufferable I do not blame you for having doubts about me due to it. Besides, perhaps it all worked out for the best. Timing is often more crucial than we imagine."

She searched his face, trying to see if he harbored any regrets or insecurities about their match, but she could find none.

"Are you saying this only because you do not want to break your word?" she asked imploringly. "Because, Gideon, I cannot live like that. I would never want you to resent me or our marriage."

"Never," he said fiercely. "I worried at first that I would be making a wrong decision one way or another, but I realize now that there is no wrong decision as long as I am with you."

"What about all of your responsibilities?" she asked. "It was the very reason we could not be together before."

"I know," he said, the first sign of concern crossing his face. "And my family's rather precarious position remains, as does all that is required of me and the people who are relying on me. But I am moving – slowly – in the right direction, and I do think that with you by my side I could get there that much faster."

Madeline took deep breaths as she tried to calm herself, hating how emotional she was becoming, but knowing that Gideon would never judge her for it.

"I will be there for you, in any way I can," she said, looking up at him, allowing the comfort and safety he always provided to wrap around her along with his embrace. "I did much for my father, and I will be of use to you, I promise. I—"

"Madeline," he stopped her, dropping a kiss on the top of her head. "You do not need to prove your worth. You need to do nothing but be you and say yes."

"Yes?"

"To me. To marrying me and spending the rest of your days with me."

"Of course," she choked out. "I thought this was going to be goodbye. But instead—"

"It is only the beginning," he finished for her before sealing his lips over hers, kissing her with such passion that he took her breath away. She wove her hands into his hair as he wrapped her tight, ending the kiss far too early for her liking, but he brushed his lips over the tip of her nose, warming it. "It is far too cold out here. Let's get you inside."

"I do not want to see anyone else," she said. "I want to stay with you, alone, for a moment, before we share all of this with everyone else."

Mischief touched his eyes – mischief she hadn't seen often upon him before, but it rather intrigued her.

He took her hand.

"Come with me."

"Where?"

"Would you like to go for a ride?"

She couldn't help the giggle that escaped.

"That sounds… like it could be fun?"

He grinned. "First, we will go to the stables."

"That wasn't the kind of ride I thought you were suggesting."

He laughed out loud before beginning to tug her forward. "That can come afterward," he said before stopping and looking at her with a much more serious expression. "I may have been on many adventures in the past, but there are none that I look forward to more than those that happen when I am with you."

She smiled. "With more to come."

"It's a promise."

CHAPTER 26

Madeline held Gideon's hand as he led her in through the stable doors. He squeezed it tight within his, content with all that they had promised one another and what was waiting for their future. His only hurdle remaining was to speak with her father, but from what she had told him in the past, he had a feeling that Lord Trenton's approval was not going to be an issue.

"Victor?" Gideon called out as they stepped through the stable doors, shutting them tightly behind him.

"Back here!" the stablehand called out before stepping out of one of the stall doors to greet them. "Lord Ashford. Lady Madeline. You look… well."

Despite his obvious efforts to hold it back, a smile stretched across his face at seeing the two of them together.

"We are going to go for a ride, Victor, if you could help us prepare the horses."

"Of course," he said. "Lady has been an excellent addition to the stables, I must say, my lord, my lady. She fits in well with the other horses and seems to enjoy it here."

"Does she now?" Gideon said, a smile tugging on his lips.

Madeline loved how ready his smile was these days, compared to the sombreness that had always been there before. "Well, perhaps we might have to arrange for her to stay with us longer."

"That would be great news to all of us."

Scout danced around their feet before going to all of the stalls and greeting the horses, who had become his friends since he had begun living at Castleton.

"It seems that Scout rather likes having her here as well," Victor noted.

"We wouldn't want to disappoint Scout," Gideon said, tugging Madeline into his side.

"No, we wouldn't," she said, shaking her head with a smile. "That settles it, I suppose."

Soon enough, the horses were saddled and Gideon and Madeline were riding away as Scout made himself comfortable with Victor and the rest of the stable. Madeline looked over at Gideon with such love in her eyes, and Gideon didn't know how he had become so lucky to have her. He wasn't sure if he *deserved* her love, but he had found it all the same.

"Would you like to race?" she asked with a grin.

"Of course," he said as they set off toward the tree line. It would be the first stop to their final destination – one that he was hoping she would be happy with.

They pushed their horses until he and Madeline were neck and neck. She was bent low over Lady, in perfect form, and he couldn't help but take a moment to admire how they moved as one. She truly was a formidable rider. Of course, riding side saddle restricted her some, but still, she was nearly out of her seat, urging her horse on.

He was so distracted that he lost focus for a moment, which was enough for her to pull ahead and beat him.

"Aha!" she called out when she made the treeline, her

cheeks flushed, her eyes bright. "I hope you did not allow me to win."

"Never," he said, shaking his head. "You are one with the horse, Madeline, truly. I never did tell you how impressive and brave it was when you escaped *Don* Rafael."

She shook her head. "It was the only way out that I could see."

"Well, I'm glad that you took it, for I must tell you, I know that I could not do this life without you. Not anymore, now that I know what it is like to have you in it with me."

She reached out, trailing her hand along his cheek as their eyes met and held.

"Where are we going?"

"Do you recall the groundskeeper's cottage?"

"I do," she said as they urged their horses forward and began walking.

"I thought perhaps we could make ourselves comfortable there. Soon enough it will be occupied again as I hope to hire him back soon."

"Gideon, that's wonderful!"

"He has done much for our family, it makes me feel like a boor for having let him go."

"You did what you thought was best. It was either him or someone else, was it not?"

He nodded. "There was nothing else to go. We spend money on almost nothing besides food for the house as well as caring for our staff and the horses. Mother hasn't had a new dress in years. It is one of the reasons she does not attend many social events." He looked up at her with a troubled look. "I'm not sure what that will mean for you, but I promise I will do my very best—"

"Gideon," she said, holding up a hand. "I told you that I will help you. I do not need a multitude of new dresses every season to feel beautiful when the way that you look at me is more than enough."

He smiled softly as they pulled up to the cottage, tying their horses on a nearby tree.

He stepped forward, taking her into his arms. "You are the most amazing treasure there could ever be. You know that, right?"

"I am beginning to," she said softly.

He led her inside the cottage, which was small and cold at the moment, but he intended to fix that. He walked over to the fireplace, finding the tinderbox before lighting it and starting the fire, as a few logs still sat in the grate.

"That should warm up in a few minutes," he said. "It's not a big room so it shouldn't take long."

He set the tinderbox down, suddenly feeling rather awkward. He didn't want to undress Madeline when it was so cold, and yet to stand here and wait—

His thoughts stopped, however, when she came behind him and wrapped her arms around his back, pressing the side of her cheek against him.

"Gideon," she whispered. "It's me."

"I know," he said. "Who else would it be?"

She laughed. "You do not have to pretend with me. I love you for who you are and I just want you to be yourself with me. Understood?"

He nodded slowly, turning around and taking her in his arms. "Understood."

"Now," she said, reaching up and placing her gloved hands against his cheeks. "Perhaps you could warm me up while we wait for the fire to do its job."

He leaned down and kissed her as he walked her backwards toward the small bed in the corner. He paused the kiss for a moment as he reached up and unclasped his cloak before spreading it over the bedcovers, lifting her, and placing her down upon it, then leaning over her and taking her lips with his.

The kiss began slowly, a gentle exploration of one another. Gideon savored the taste of Madeline, a mixture of peppermint from her breath and the subtle sweetness that was uniquely her own. He traced the outline of her lips with his tongue, teasing and coaxing them to part for him.

Madeline responded eagerly, deepening the kiss, her gloved hands sliding down from his cheeks to his neck, where she tugged at the buttons of his jacket. A shiver ran through Gideon as her touch brought warmth to his skin. His fingers moved to the clasp of her cloak, freeing it before removing the shawl she had donned underneath. He had no idea if it was still cold in the room, for he was being filled with heat that came from deep within.

Their kisses grew more fervent, ignited by the passion that had been smoldering between them. Gideon had expected that the first time he had made love to Madeline would have satisfied his desire, but he had been wrong – it had only fueled it.

His lips moved from hers to trace a path along her jawline, peppering soft, lingering kisses along the way. He relished how her breath hitched and quickened against his cheek.

Madeline's hands roamed over Gideon's body, tracing the contours of his chest and slipping beneath the fabric of his shirt. Her touch ignited a fire within his veins and he moaned softly against her skin as her fingertips wandered across his abdomen, leaving a trail of tingling sensations in their wake.

Desire consumed him, and he yearned to feel every inch of her. With gentle yet firm hands, Gideon cupped her face, his thumbs caressing her cheeks as he deepened the kiss. Their mouths moved in perfect harmony, tongues intertwining and exploring, their breath melding together in a symphony.

Senses heightened, Gideon's touch grew more urgent, the tips of his fingers skimming along the curve of Madeline's waist before gliding upward to slowly unfasten the trail of buttons along her spine. When he achieved his aim, he slid the sleeves down her arms before the garment slipped from her shoulders like a whisper, revealing the delicate lines of her figure and leaving her clad only in her stays, thin chemise, and the soft glow of the fire.

Gideon's heart raced as he absorbed the sight of Madeline, her skin glowing with the flickers of light behind her.

He lowered himself onto the bed beside her, his fingers trembling with anticipation. Gideon marveled at the softness of her skin beneath his touch, at the way it yielded to him as if made solely for his hands. The warmth of their bodies mingled, creating a cocoon that enveloped them in a world of their own. The cabin could still have been freezing and Gideon would not have had any awareness of it.

Locking eyes with Madeline, he finally understood what she meant when she said he could be himself with her, that there was nothing he couldn't share. "I love you, Madeline. You are the fortune that I was looking for. Who would have thought it would take an entire treasure hunt to find the woman who was right in front of me the whole time?"

A smile played on her lips as she reached out to trace invisible patterns on his chest.

"It's as you said," she said softly. "Maybe we needed those clues along the way to help us determine who we really were and what we each truly needed."

Gideon's heart swelled with affection as he watched Madeline's fingers skim across his ribs. Her touch was gentle, yet nothing had ever had a stronger effect upon him. He reveled in the way her eyes sparkled with love and trust, mirroring his own emotions.

"I love you too, Gideon," Madeline whispered, her voice a soft caress against his ear. "You've brought light into my life like no other and have shown me what love truly means. Never before have I felt so cherished, truly. Before now, I have never been someone's first choice, but the fact that you chose me over anything else, even when all seemed so much more consequential, has proven to me what love truly means."

"When someone becomes your reason for existing… nothing else much matters," he said, laying his entire soul bare before her.

Their words hung in the air, mingling with the warmth of the fire that crackled nearby. Everything outside of this cabin faded away, leaving only the two of them, which, Gideon realized, was what mattered the most. Everything else would come as long as the two of them were together.

As their hands explored one another, Gideon marveled at the way Madeline responded to his touch. Her skin seemed to come alive under his fingertips. Every gasp, every sigh that escaped her lips fueled his desire to please her, to make her feel cherished and adored.

Madeline's fingers traced gentle paths over Gideon's broad shoulders, her touch sensuous and tender, at odds with the dangerous spark of fire in her eyes as she gazed up at him, her lips parting slightly in anticipation. She whispered his name, a soft yet sultry plea that sent a ripple of desire through him.

He moved closer, his lips brushing against the sensitive skin of her neck, savoring the taste of her. Her breath hitched, and she arched her back, pressing her body against his, a silent plea to be closer, to feel the fire of his skin against hers.

"I need you, Gideon," she breathed, her voice breathy. "Here, now, and always."

He groaned softly, his hands gripping her waist, pulling her even farther into his embrace. As his lips found hers once again, he could feel the heat of her desire, potent and passionate.

Her hips swayed in rhythm to the motion of their kiss, her face flushed with desire, her eyes half-lidded as she gazed up at him.

"Don't stop," she whispered, her voice barely more than a breath.

"Never," he replied fiercely. Her fingers threaded through his hair, holding him close as their bodies continued to move against each other, a dance of lust and love as old as time.

As their bodies mingled, their breathing became ragged and uneven. Their hearts pounded in unison, matching the rhythm of their movements. The air thickened with the scent of their passion, the scent irresistibly intoxicating.

Gideon's hands traced the curve of Madeline's hips, his fingers dancing along the line of her waist, and then lower still. He felt her tremble as he held her closer, her skin warming under his touch.

Madeline's fingers threaded through Gideon's hair, pulling him closer as their lips met once more. This time, their kiss was deeper, more primitive, more intense. As her tongue tangled with his, she whispered his name and it nearly sent him over the edge right there but he was able to hold himself back to see to her pleasure first.

He shifted back on the bed, leaning against the wall as he lifted her, gripping the firm swell of her bottom as she wrapped her legs around his hips. He began rocking her against him, back and forth, sliding her over his cock, closing his eyes and throwing his head back with a groan.

"I'm ready," she said, and on her next rock backward she

reached down and notched him against her before sliding him home.

"Gideon!" she cried out as she continued her movements, her strong legs pushing her forward and back along with his help, her pelvis grinding into his.

Perspiration beaded on his brow as she moved, and he knew that he would never tire of this, of her, for the rest of their lives. He had no idea what this woman was doing to him, but whatever it was, he couldn't have asked for anything more.

Her movements became more urgent, more frenzied, as she began to tighten around him and he knew she was close.

He reached up and tweaked her nipples, which seemed to be what she needed as she was soon calling his name even louder, pulsing around him, causing his world to explode with hers as he spent into her.

When their movements finally came to a stop, she collapsed onto him, her head in the crook of his neck as her heavy breathing matched his while they stayed locked together.

"I cannot wait until we can do this every night," he said with a sigh, brushing his hand down her hair.

"Soon enough," she said softly. "It is hard to believe how fast everything can change."

"Are you staying, then?" he asked as she lifted her head to look at him. "Or are you returning to London first?"

He wasn't sure he could bear the thought of being apart from her for even a short period of time, but if that was what she wished, he would wait. He would wait as long as she needed him to.

"That depends."

"On?" he said, hope sparking in his chest.

"On how soon you would like to be married," she said with a small smile.

Gideon grinned. "The moment we have everything in order," he said. "It's time I go speak with your father."

Her smile matched his. "Agreed."

They found their clothing, helping one another, as playful in redressing each other as they had been when they had undressed.

Gideon's breath caught as he watched her. She was more beautiful than anything he ever could have imagined in his life, but even more so, she fit him in ways he could never have guessed.

That, he supposed, was what love was.

And nothing could ever make him let it go again.

CHAPTER 27

Madeline was not surprised that her father was completely thrilled by Gideon's request for her hand.

"What did you do to him, girl?" he asked her after, and she had to stop herself from rolling her eyes that he wouldn't think that she alone was enough to cause a man to want to marry her.

"He loves me for me, Father," she said, telling the truth. "Which should make you happy."

"It does, of course it does," he said, setting his shoulders as though he was the one who had captured such a prize. "A duke in the family. My goodness."

"I do have one request," she said, turning to her father and stopping in front of the dining room doors before they walked in with the rest of the guests for dinner. "Please do not do anything to bring further scandal to this family. They have been through enough and they are good people who deserve to be celebrated.

"Me, scandalous?" he said, placing a hand on his chest in mock horror. "Never."

Madeline rolled her eyes as she caught Gideon's eye from across the room, knowing that, no matter what her father did, Gideon wouldn't hold it against her. They could count on one another to stand together, no matter what was to come.

Her father left the next day, as he had planned. Madeline stood in the foyer, watching him ride away, a strange sense of nostalgia as well as relief coming over her. She loved her father, truly she did, but she knew that she had been a burden to him, despite their love for one another and all that he had taught her.

She sensed Gideon's presence behind her before she heard or felt him, and soon his arms came around her waist, his mouth nuzzling into her neck, which she leaned into.

"Are you not afraid that someone might see us?" she asked.

"What does it matter?" he said. "Our servants have certainly proven their loyalty and our friends do not hide their affection when they are here."

"True," she said with a laugh that quickly died away when she thought of the future. "I will miss them when they all return home."

"I know," he said. "They have all noted their intention to stay until our wedding and then they will return to their prospective estates. Do you think your father will be here to see us wed?"

She shrugged. "It is not as though we are particularly far from London, and he loves the ride so it is possible. Whether he will choose to make the time for it or not is another question."

"Does that trouble you?"

"No," she said truthfully, turning in his arms. "I have you and the rest of our friends, who are my chosen family now."

"We most certainly are," Cassandra said as she walked

into the foyer, Devon behind her. "Well, you and I were always family, but now you have the rest of us too. We all do. I believe it is time that we properly celebrate your engagement and the end of this treasure hunt, what do you think?"

"I think that is a brilliant idea," Devon said, even as Gideon was shaking his head.

"A nice dinner will be enough."

"Gideon," Madeline said, tilting her head. "We are at Castleton. A nice dinner might not entirely be part of our plans."

"Actually," he said, with an incline of his head. "I have a surprise. Anderson told me his sister was looking for work, and, as it happens, she is a cook. A good one too," he said at Cassandra's skeptical look. "I spoke to Mother about it and she was infinitely relieved. In the meantime, Hattie has expressed her desire to be a lady's maid, to which I am told by the housekeeper she will be much more suited. As you told me that yours would prefer to return home closer to her family—"

"She can be mine," Madeline said with a smile. "Perfect."

"I feel as though you are already part of Castleton," Gideon said as the four of them began walking together to the drawing room, where the rest of their friends awaited. "Mother will likely spend more time here in the country as well, now that she doesn't need to be in London with Cassandra for the Season. We will split our time with my Parliamentary obligations but she spends so much of her time with Father that I am sure she would love to have you take on some of the household duties."

"She most certainly would," Cassandra said holding out a small glass to Madeline that she had collected from the sideboard of the drawing room, where the drinks had already been poured and awaited them.

It seemed that this party was happening whether Gideon

wanted it to or not. His demeanor was relaxed, however, and Madeline had the feeling that as much as he protested, he was happy to be free of his obligations – for one night, at least.

Madeline felt a touch on her elbow and she turned, finding Faith standing behind her.

"Madeline, could I speak to you for a moment?"

"Of course."

They moved off to the side and Faith reached out and took her hand.

"I need to offer you an apology," she said.

"Whatever for?"

"For being uncertain about you and Gideon. I was wrong. Seeing the two of you together, it is obvious how much you love one another and how you complement one another well. I should know better than to assume opposites would not work well together."

She smiled in recognition of her own marriage, and Madeline patted the top of her hand.

"You were only looking out for me, which I appreciate. But thank you."

Faith smiled gratefully at her before Devon called out their names.

"A toast!" Devon said, waving all of them forward, until the ten of them stood in a circle in the middle of the drawing room, glasses held up before them. Gideon wrapped his free hand around Madeline's waist, holding her against him, her back to his front.

"Gideon, would you like to do the honors?" Devon asked, and Gideon lifted his drink toward him.

"You start," he said. "I will finish."

"Very well," Devon said with a grin. "It is hard to believe that we are standing here together, celebrating the end of this treasure hunt. Not only did we find a fortune – one that we are, quite sadly, returning from where it came – but we grew friendships and romances, each of us finding the person with whom we will spend the rest of our lives. I do not believe that any of this would ever have come about had we not encountered these circumstances with one another. We faced danger, peril, and what seemed to be, at times, impossible clues and situations, but here we are at the end of it all. Gideon?"

"I could not ask for better friends," he said, looking around at them all, needing each of them to understand just how true his words were. "Not many people would take such a leap and believe in what I presented to you, let alone put such effort into doing this simply for the sake of helping me. I appreciate it more than you will ever know." He had to pause for a moment to prevent the emotion from spilling over. "Little could I imagine what true fortune was awaiting me." He squeezed Madeline's hip. "To friends, and to the family that we have all become."

He lifted his drink, as did the rest of them, a tear or two present on the faces of each of them.

"That was beautiful," Ferrington said with a sniff after they had set their glasses down.

"The speeches or the drink?" Whitehall asked.

"Both," Ferrington said with a sigh. "That is some damn fine brandy."

"Courtesy of Covington here," Gideon said, hoping that someday Castleton would be able to supply something similar.

"It's very good," Percy said with a smile. She would know – she considered herself a connoisseur of such spirits.

After a time, the women came to settle around the table in the middle of the room, sitting back with another brandy, this one from Castleton's stores and one that was better to drink after the first had warmed the body.

Cassandra looked around at all of them with wonder in her eyes. "When I found that riddle, I was certainly not expecting that we would all be sitting here, married – or almost married – women," she said with a laugh. "Do you think my great-grandparents had any idea at the time of what a nuisance this treasure hunting would be?"

Madeline knew that Cassandra was joking, but still, she considered the question seriously.

"I think they did, actually," she said. "They likely wanted the person to find the treasure to be someone who would go to the effort required to return it. The only way to ensure they found the right people was to put them through such a rigorous treasure hunt that they would have to be the determined sort to finish it."

"Or the sort with good friends," Faith said wryly, to which they laughed.

"Or both," Hope added.

"It gives me an idea," Cassandra said, a twist to her smile that told Madeline she was thinking of something rather wicked.

"What is it?" she couldn't help but ask.

"We should create a treasure hunt of our own," Cassandra said. "One for our descendants to discover."

"I love it," Percy said excitedly, sitting up straighter. "We could each take some of the clues, and they would be connected. Then maybe someday, our descendants could find one another, if, for whatever reason, they had come to be separated."

"Shall we tell the men?" Madeline asked, but Cassandra was already shaking her head, a wicked smile gracing her lips.

"Not yet," she said. "Just like this riddle, let us see what we can do with it first before we bring them into it."

"Do you think they have thought of the same idea already?" Hope asked.

"No," Cassandra said. "I think they are still trying to overcome all that we have gone through. Men can't seem to handle it quite the way that we can, can they?"

They laughed at that before Cassandra looked back at all of them. "So, now that the adventure is over, shall we return to the adventures of our books?"

"How will we continue our book club if we are all days away from one another at our respective estates?" Faith asked.

"I figured that we can read while we are in the country, and then meet when we are in London. We could also, perhaps, send one another our thoughts through letters. It will help us feel connected when we are apart."

"I like that," Madeline said before she grinned. "I believe it is my turn to pick the next book."

"Absolutely not," Cassandra said, shaking her head. "You choose the *worst* stories. All emotional and they never end up together. That is not the type of romance that we agreed to read."

"You never know," Madeline said impishly, "perhaps I have changed and will choose something different this time."

"Gideon has changed you?"

"It's not that," she said, looking at all of them before her gaze caught on the man across the room, who had changed her perspective on so much of life. "It's that I now believe in happy endings."

EPILOGUE

*G*ideon loved Castleton in the summer.

He loved it all year round, of course, but the grounds and gardens were unlike any others he had seen and he was particularly pleased with how they were looking now that the groundskeeper had returned.

Burt was taking great care in returning them to their former glory, and Gideon stood now, surveying the grounds before him.

Madeline stood beside him, her hand in his as they took it all in.

"Shall we walk?" she asked, and he nodded, swinging her hand in his.

"Let's."

They walked in comfortable silence for a few minutes, Scout bounding in front of them, running ahead and then back as though urging them to keep up, past the water fountain, which was running once more, down the path and toward the ruins, which were one part of the grounds that remained as they always did.

THE HEIR'S FORTUNE

"It's beautiful," Madeline mused, looking around them. "No longer perfectly overgrown and formidable enough to be a setting for one of my gothic novels."

"A pity," he said, tsking and she laughed.

"I suppose you could say that." She looked up at him. "Thank you for taking the time to walk with me this morning. I know how hard you have been working."

"Of course," he said. "I will always take time for you. Besides, none of this would have been possible without you."

"I can hardly take the credit," she murmured, although her cheeks turned slightly pink.

"It's true," he insisted. "I spent so long trying to improve on the way we had done things before when you made me realize that we had to do things a *different* way. A better way."

"Who would have thought that my father and his laziness would have helped us?"

"Perhaps he is smarter than us all," Gideon said with a laugh.

Gideon had been musing one day on the fact that Madeline's father spent so much time away from his own property. It was not nearly as expansive as Castleton's land and village, but he still had much to care for.

Madeline had told him that he had done so by diversifying his land, investing in innovations that required less labour, and hiring men to look after things for him.

Of course, Gideon had no interest in divesting his responsibilities upon another – that was how they had ended up in this mess, after all – but it did urge him to start to think about how they could better utilize the land.

As Madeline had helped her father research all of the different ways he could make more money with less time, she was rather knowledgeable about options available to them, and Gideon had already begun implementing some ideas on crop rotation and had started to invest what he could into some innovations that showed promise.

"I have a surprise for you."

"A surprise? Out here?"

He nodded, taking her hand and tugging her toward the stables, his pulse picking up when he imagined what she might think about what awaited them.

"Are we going for a ride?"

"No."

"Are we going to see Lady?"

"No, but of course we can check in on her."

"Then what—"

She stopped suddenly when she saw the men before them, along with the timber that was piled high beside the stable.

"What are they doing?"

"They are building an attachment onto the stable."

"Whatever for?"

"We are going to need more room, once you begin your equine training."

Madeline's jaw dropped as her eyes began to burn with the tears that threatened her.

"You—you are building me a place to train horses?"

"Yes," he said, turning to her, wiping away the solitary tear that had escaped. "This is what you wanted, is it not? To be able to train your own horses, you said?"

"Yes, but I hardly thought you would remember, let alone do anything about it. It is very untoward—"

He leaned down and kissed her, stopping her words.

"If there is anything I have learned in the past year, it is not to be concerned about what other people might think. I want you to be happy, and if this will make you happy, then have whatever you please. I thought I would also invite a trainer to come work with you until you are comfortable training yourself, if you would like that?"

"I would love that," she said, melting into him. "Thank you, Gideon. Not only for this but in loving me for exactly who I am."

Gideon was pleased that the smile didn't fall from her face as they returned to the house until they came close enough to hear a shout and they quickened their steps when they saw Anderson awaiting them.

"Anderson?" Gideon said, his heart beginning to pound with concern that something had happened to his father. "Is all well?"

"Yes, my lord," Anderson said, a smile broadening on his face. "More than well."

Gideon waited, lifting a brow.

"I have received word from my relatives. The treasure arrived safely back in Peru."

"Wonderful," Gideon said, relieved. He had been worried that they should have heard something by now. "Were Lord and Lady Ferrington well?"

"They were," Anderson confirmed.

Once Anderson had arranged for the treasure to be returned, only one problem remained – they were not sure who they could trust to see it there safely. That's when Ferrington and Faith decided that they had enjoyed their first adventure to Spain so much that they would like to sail together once more. They were set to return shortly.

"There is something else," Anderson said, and Gideon became wary once more.

"Yes?"

"They said they sent something back with Lord and Lady Ferrington."

"What is it?"

"A few pieces of the treasure – to remember this all by, and to thank you for what you have done."

Gideon and Madeline exchanged a look.

"What does *a few pieces* mean?" he asked.

"From the sounds of it, perhaps a trunk."

Gideon's jaw dropped open as Madeline's grip on his arm tightened. "Do you know what this means?" he asked her, finding that her eyes were as wide as his own.

"It means that everything you have wanted – for the estate, for your people – can come true right away, and not in time. You can give back to all those who helped you along the way."

"Is that fair for us to take, though?" he asked, scratching his head. "It doesn't belong to us."

"To return it would be to insult the gesture they have made for you," Anderson said. "It's yours."

"An interesting turn of events," he murmured.

"Anything you need, my lord, please let me know."

"Of course, Anderson."

Gideon turned, staring out over the grounds of Castleton as the large estate stretched out in front of him. It had always been and always would be home, no matter its condition.

And yet, it was so much better to have someone to share it with. To share all of this with.

"You are a treasure, Madeline," he said, wrapping his arms around her.

"As are you," she said. "A man who finally knows his worth."

"The hunt is over," he said. "But I have a feeling the adventure has only just begun."

THE END

* * *

Dear reader,

I hope you enjoyed Gideon and Madeline's story, as well as the entire Reckless Rogues series! I cannot believe that we are saying goodbye to these characters, who have taken up such residence in my head. I knew from the beginning that we would start with Cassandra's story and Gideon's would be last, but I wasn't entirely sure where the adventure in between would take us. These characters had such distinct personalities and really spoke to me.

I would love to know what you thought of them all! You are always welcome to email me at ellie@elliestclair.com, post in my facebook group or, of course, leave a review.

If you would like a little more time with our lords and ladies, you can download an extended epilogue about what life looks like for them five years in the future here: The Heir's Fortune Extended Epilogue.

In the meantime, if you love some mystery sprinkled in with your romance and haven't yet read my Remingtons of the Regency series, then be sure to start with The Mystery of the Debonair Duke!

Or, if you'd like a little taste of what's next from me, then keep reading for a preview of Her Runaway Duke.

If you haven't yet signed up for my newsletter, I would love to have you join us! You will receive Unmasking a Duke for free, as well as links to giveaways, sales, new releases, and stories about my coffee addiction, my struggle to keep my plants alive, and how much trouble one loveable wolf-looka-like dog can get into.

<u>www.elliestclair.com/ellies-newsletter</u>

Or you can join my Facebook group, Ellie St. Clair's Ever Afters, and stay in touch daily.

Until next time, happy reading!

With love,

Ellie

HER RUNAWAY DUKE - CHAPTER ONE

"You cannot marry him. I will not allow it."

Siena straightened from her slump and sent a regretful smile toward Eliza, who stood, arms crossed and shoulders set as though ready to do battle, a few feet away.

"If only you were the one who was making the decision."

"I have no idea how your parents could expect you to marry a man so... distasteful. Unsettling. *Old*. He must be older than your father. And the way he looks at you—"

"Is how a husband is allowed to look at his wife, I would suspect," Siena said, although she couldn't help but shiver at the thought of Lord Mulberry touching her, let alone—no. She couldn't think of it, or she would never get through this day.

It wasn't his age that bothered her. It was how he made her feel. Eliza wasn't wrong.

"I suppose the only positive of this situation is that he might not last much longer," Eliza said as she stood from her seat in the armchair before the fire and walked over to stand behind Siena, meeting her gaze in the mirror of the vanity.

Siena's lady's maid had already come and gone, having

prepared her for the morning wedding ceremony, and only Eliza remained as they waited for the carriage to convey them to the church.

Siena's eyes widened. "Eliza!"

Her best friend shrugged, her blue-green eyes alighting with mischief as her dimples played in her cheeks. "It's the truth."

She reached out and stole a lily from the bouquet sitting on the vanity top in front of them and tucked it into a pin that was holding Siena's blonde hair in an intricately braided style that was far more elaborate than she preferred.

But it didn't matter, for who would ever see it but her family, her groom, and his children?

"Children" who were older than she was.

"How your parents could do this to you, I will never understand," Eliza said, shaking her head with her hands on her hips. Siena knew that Eliza meant well, but it was easy to say such things when one had parents allowed her to do as she pleased.

"They are most concerned that I am well looked after," Siena said softly.

"You are too kind. I suppose it doesn't hurt that your new husband's family is so well respected in social circles," Eliza added in a jaded tone.

"I suppose not," Siena admitted, looking up and meeting Eliza's eyes, noting the pity in her friend's gaze.

"You do not have to do this, you know," Eliza murmured, and hope sprang in Siena's chest before she could tamp it down.

"What other choice do I have?" Siena said, throwing her hands up to the side. "I have asked my parents for more time to find another suitor, but they have no interest in hearing my thoughts. This is how it has to be, whether I like it or not."

"There is always another option," Eliza said slowly. "You just might have to take a risk." She looked from one side to the other, as though someone might hear her. "If you want to escape, I will help you."

"*Escape?*" Siena stood, startled. "How? And where would I possibly go?"

"Anywhere," Eliza said, reaching out and taking Siena's hands in hers, more fervent now. "I have a plan. I wasn't sure if you would agree, but just in case, everything is prepared, including a horse with saddlebags packed. I do not live far and my father won't notice a horse missing from his stable for a time."

"That would be stealing!"

"That is what you are most concerned with right now?" Eliza said with a sigh. "Honestly, Siena, do you always have to do what is right, what you are told? Your selflessness is to be admired, but it also drives me mad."

Siena hated the shame that washed through her at Eliza's words, especially as she knew her friend was right.

"If I do not marry Lord Mulberry," she began, as that hope began to rise in her throat once more, "then no one will ever have me. I will be ostracized and then I will never have what I truly want."

"Which is?"

"To be a mother," Siena said softly.

Eliza's eyes bore into hers. "You do understand what you have to do to become a mother, do you not? Or should I remind you? For it is very important that you know before you marry Lord Mulberry."

"Of course I know," Siena said. "You have shared with my all of your 'knowledge' before."

"Just making sure," Eliza said. "You make it sound as though I have experience when really it is all from studying—"

She was interrupted by a knock at the door before Siena's lady's maid, Alice, opened it a crack.

"My lady, it is time for you to proceed to the church."

"Thank you, Alice," Siena said before dropping Eliza's hands. "We should go. I do thank you, Eliza. You are like a sister to me. I know you are looking out for me in what you feel is best."

"Someone has to do it," Eliza said grimly, "for you certainly do not look out for yourself."

Eliza's words stayed with Siena as they left the house on Grosvenor Square and entered the carriage, where her mother was already waiting, her face set in disapproval.

"I do hope that you shall be more attentive to your husband," she said with a sniff. Siena ignored her, used to her barbed remarks, although she could sense Eliza balking behind her.

"Where is Father?" Siena asked, dropping her lilac skirts around her as she and Eliza took a seat across from her mother. She hoped Eliza wouldn't say anything to anger her mother. Eliza's parents were of proper enough standing for the daughters to be friends, but Siena's mother did not hide her disapproval for the outspoken Eliza – nor Eliza her disdain for Siena's mother, who had always been the domineering sort.

While Siena wouldn't have to obey her for much longer, she knew she was only trading one puppet master for another.

The closer they drew to the church, the faster her heart began to pound. While she hadn't been particularly pleased about the marriage her father had arranged, she had tried to ignore it until now, knowing that there was nothing she could do to stop it so what was the point in worrying over it? She had tried in vain to appeal to her brother, but he was merely her father's mimic and was happy to marry her off so that he would never have the risk of looking after her.

This wedding was inevitable now, and the closer they drew to St. George's, the more perspiration broke out on her brow at the reality that the next hour would change the rest of her life.

Her heart was beating so hard it was nearly pounding out of her chest, and her vision threatened to blacken completely. As the panic set in, she looked to Eliza, and her friend, understanding her better than anyone, set her lips in a firm line before reaching out and squeezing Siena's hand. She lifted a brow, asking Siena what she wanted to do.

Siena only paused for a moment before she nodded just once, clenching her jaw.

She had always done what she was told, had never taken a chance or done anything for herself. Everything she did was to make those around her happy.

But not today.

She would do it.

She would escape this wedding.

* * *

"Would you like me to light the fire, your grace?"

"No."

Levi sat in the worn navy damask chair in front of the empty hearth, staring into where flames should have been flickering, warming him and the room.

Which they would have were he a different man, one without his demons.

"It is rather cold—"

"Light the rooms you are using if that will keep you warm, Thornbury."

"I am not concerned for myself, your grace, but the staff—"

"Light the rooms for them, then. Leave this one."

"Very good, your grace."

The butler closed the door softly behind him, leaving Levi alone in the drawing room, dark but for the light from behind the three large windows. On the rare sunny day, the room would be alight, but today, on a day as gloomy as his mood, it simply cast a blue glow around the room, although it was enough to read the paper before him.

He should have ended his subscription months ago, but he found that he could not completely shut himself off from the outside world.

The article was small, on the bottom right side of the third page. Most readers probably skimmed over it, no longer interested. But the fact that it remained was enough to irk him. When would they be done with him?

The door opened with a creak once more, causing Levi to throw the paper down in exasperation.

"Your grace?" Thronebury had been with him long enough that he did not shrink away from his tempers, although Levi somewhat wished that he did.

"I told you, Thornbury, I do not want a fire."

"It is not that, your grace. You have a visitor."

Still facing away from the door, Levi sighed as he rubbed his fingers against his temples. "Tell Fitz to go away."

"I had a feeling you would say that," came his friend's far-too-jovial voice from behind him. "So I showed myself in. Thank you, Thornbury. I appreciate your attempt at properly announcing me."

"Lord Fitzroy," Thornbury murmured before the door shut with a click behind him.

Levi tried to surreptitiously place the scandal sheet in the book next to him, but Fitz was too fast. Levi envied the light, unburdened skip in his step as he took a seat in the chair next to him, reaching out and snatching an untouched sandwich from the tray on the table between them.

"Still reading that shit, I see?"

"It is drivel, yes, but drivel people read," Levi muttered. "Why will they not leave me be?"

"It is not every day a man survives your experience, ascends to the highest ranks, and then responds by hiding himself away in a run-down estate outside of London," Fitz said, crossing one knee over the other and then bouncing it up and down. The man could never sit still, always moving in one way or another.

"You make it sound as though I am someone to be admired."

"You are."

Levi snorted. His friend couldn't have been further from the truth.

"I came to share a thought with you."

"A letter would have sufficed."

"And miss this electrifying conversation? What a shame that would be. Besides, how would I know that you would open and read what I had to say?"

Levi remained silent, for Fitz had a point.

"You have been in hiding long enough. It has been over a year and, as you say, there is still much speculation as to what has become of you. A man becomes a duke and suddenly disappears? Many think you are dead, you know."

"Let them," he said before adding, "They also think I'm a murderer. Not sure which is worse."

"No one is saying that much anymore. The issue is, you have done nothing to rebuild the entailed estate and you have a dukedom that could sorely use you, Levi."

"They do not need me. Others are seeing to it."

"It's not enough," Fitz said, leaning forward, his elbows on his thighs as looked closer at Levi, but Levi refused to meet his gaze.

"What is this 'thought' of yours?" Levi asked, wanting to be done with this. He both loved and hated Fitz's visits. As much as he enjoyed seeing his oldest friend, he also hated that they always brought him a spark of hope that life could go back to the way it used to be.

That, however, was impossible.

"It has been long enough. If you return to London and society and show your face, then all the rumors will be put to rest and no one will talk any longer. It will also be much better for you than sitting here in this awful mausoleum. Did you know it is freezing in here? And I am not talking about just the temperature, although that is also an issue. When was this place built? Surely there was another in your possession you could have chosen, although I do appreciate how close to London you are, for I enjoy the ride."

Levi looked at him, blinking as he tried to sift through all of the nonsense that had come out of Fitz's mouth.

"You think I should show my face in London? *My* face?" His mouth dropped open. "Surely you are jesting."

"I would never jest," Fitz said, pausing a moment before bursting into laughter, although Levi remained straight-faced. "Very well. I would jest. But not about this. What are you going to do, Levi, sit here alone staring at the wall for the rest of your days? How morbidly depressing."

"It fits, doesn't it?"

"You need heirs."

"No, I don't," Levi shrugged. "I do not much care about my family line, and someone will take over what is left of the mess that remains."

"Is that any way to honor your family?"

"They are not here to care," he said, pausing a moment before adding, "nor will I be when an heir becomes an issue."

His words were true, but there was more to it. To have children, he would need a wife. While he was sure that some poor woman could be forced to marry him for his title alone, he was not about to saddle anyone with the horror of staring at him for the rest of her life.

He had no choice.

He would remain here in hiding. Alone. As it should be.

Her Runaway Duke will be available on Amazon and in Kindle Unlimited.

ALSO BY ELLIE ST. CLAIR

Reckless Rogues
The Earls's Secret
The Viscount's Code
The Scholar's Key
The Lord's Compass
The Heir's Fortune

Noble Pursuits
Her Runaway Duke

The Remingtons of the Regency
The Mystery of the Debonair Duke
The Secret of the Dashing Detective
The Clue of the Brilliant Bastard
The Quest of the Reclusive Rogue

The Unconventional Ladies
Lady of Mystery
Lady of Fortune
Lady of Providence
Lady of Charade

The Unconventional Ladies Box Set

To the Time of the Highlanders
A Time to Wed

A Time to Love

A Time to Dream

Thieves of Desire

The Art of Stealing a Duke's Heart

A Jewel for the Taking

A Prize Worth Fighting For

Gambling for the Lost Lord's Love

Romance of a Robbery

Thieves of Desire Box Set

The Bluestocking Scandals

[Designs on a Duke](#)

[Inventing the Viscount](#)

[Discovering the Baron](#)

[The Valet Experiment](#)

[Writing the Rake](#)

[Risking the Detective](#)

[A Noble Excavation](#)

[A Gentleman of Mystery](#)

The Bluestocking Scandals Box Set: Books 1-4

The Bluestocking Scandals Box Set: Books 5-8

Blooming Brides

A Duke for Daisy

A Marquess for Marigold

An Earl for Iris

A Viscount for Violet

The Blooming Brides Box Set: Books 1-4

Happily Ever After
The Duke She Wished For
Someday Her Duke Will Come
Once Upon a Duke's Dream
He's a Duke, But I Love Him
Loved by the Viscount
Because the Earl Loved Me

Happily Ever After Box Set Books 1-3
Happily Ever After Box Set Books 4-6

The Victorian Highlanders
Duncan's Christmas - (prequel)
Callum's Vow
Finlay's Duty
Adam's Call
Roderick's Purpose
Peggy's Love

The Victorian Highlanders Box Set Books 1-5

Searching Hearts
Duke of Christmas (prequel)
Quest of Honor
Clue of Affection
Hearts of Trust
Hope of Romance
Promise of Redemption

Searching Hearts Box Set (Books 1-5)

Standalones

Always Your Love

The Stormswept Stowaway

A Touch of Temptation

Unmasking a Duke

Christmas Books

A Match Made at Christmas

A Match Made in Winter

Christmastide with His Countess

Her Christmas Wish

Merry Misrule

Duke of Christmas

Duncan's Christmas

For a full list of all of Ellie's books, please see www.elliestclair.com/books.

ABOUT THE AUTHOR

Ellie has always loved reading, writing, and history. For many years she has written short stories, non-fiction, and has worked on her true love and passion -- romance novels.

In every era there is the chance for romance, and Ellie enjoys exploring many different time periods, cultures, and geographic locations. No matter when or where, love can always prevail. She has a particular soft spot for the bad boys of history, and loves a strong heroine in her stories.

Ellie and her husband love nothing more than spending time at home with their children and Husky cross. Ellie can typically be found at the lake in the summer, pushing the stroller all year round, and, of course, with her computer in her lap or a book in hand.

She also loves corresponding with readers, so be sure to contact her!

www.elliestclair.com
ellie@elliestclair.com

- facebook.com/elliestclairauthor
- x.com/ellie_stclair
- instagram.com/elliestclairauthor
- amazon.com/author/elliestclair
- goodreads.com/elliestclair
- bookbub.com/authors/elliest.clair
- pinterest.com/elliestclair

Printed in Great Britain
by Amazon